The Treasure Canyon

Twice a year old Jake Cotter would disappear dressed like a prospector and return to put money and nuggets in the bank. Jealous neighbours decided that his sudden wealth must have come from a secret goldmine and it wasn't very long before Jake paid for his secret with his life. Now his son Tom has returned to the scene to avenge his father.

In a series of wild encounters he too becomes a target for the greedy killers and finally discovers that just one man is behind his problems. His bitter quest for truth and justice is destined to end in a treasure hunt of lethal proportions. Will he also pay with his life?

The Treasure Canyon

TOM BENSON

A Black Horse Western

ROBERT HALE · LONDON

© Tom Benson 2001
First published in Great Britain 2001

ISBN 0 7090 6938 3

Robert Hale Limited
Clerkenwell House
Clerkenwell Green
London EC1R 0HT

Typeset by
Derek Doyle & Associates, Liverpool.
Printed and bound in Great Britain by
Antony Rowe Limited, Wiltshire.

One

There were seven wagons entering the narrow trail that lay between two low canyon walls of multicoloured sandstone. It was a dried-up river bed littered with coarse scrub from which frightened jack rabbits ran for cover at the noise made by the intruders. There were two men on each wagon – one driving the large horses, the other nursing a rifle across his knees. They wore the uniforms of the United States army, dust-covered to a dirty grey that blended with the once white covers of the wagons.

There was also a cavalry escort. Six men and a young lieutenant who rode their mounts cautiously over the broken ground. The first four wagons were each drawn by two animals while the others had four horses to pull them. There were water barrels strapped to the sides and the iron-shod wheels crushed the sandy gravel with sharp, cracking noises that echoed from the low walls of the canyon.

It was near the end of the narrow trail, and just when the sandstone walls were fading away towards open ground, that a volley of gunfire shattered the warm air.

The driver of the first wagon pitched from his seat while his companion made a wild grab at the falling reins. He missed them and leaned over to apply the brake lever. As he pulled at it desperately, another shot took him in the chest and he fell down between the moving horses.

The other drivers and guards were having the same problems. Some were wounded, others killed outright by the hail of fire that came from the rocks and from the top of the canyon.

The soldiers on horseback tried to control their mounts but the shots were hitting men and animals. The young lieutenant was among the first to fall. He had drawn his pistol but took a bullet in the side of the head before he could even cock the weapon. His horse galloped off towards the far end of the trail and vanished from sight.

It was all over in about three minutes. Hardly a shot was fired by the military as the hidden attackers showered lead at them from the safety of their positions. Bullets and buckshot had done a lethal job.

All the cavalrymen were dead or dying, and only two of the wagon drivers still held the reins of their restless and frightened animals. They stood frozen, each controlling the horses with one hand while the other was raised as a token of surrender. There was a silence as wisps of acrid smoke curled over the scene, while the groans of the injured sounded loud after the burst of noise. The pawing of a horse on the rocky earth seemed to echo from the low walls of the canyon as the startled birds began to settle again on the low bushes and craggy ledges.

A figure emerged from a group of rocks. He carried a shotgun that he waved at the two drivers to indicate that they should climb down from their wagons. They obeyed hurriedly while several other men appeared along the ridges and from the bushes that sprouted from the poor soil.

The man with the shotgun advanced on the drivers. He was in his forties, with a mean, thin face and crooked grin as he levelled the weapon. He pulled the triggers in quick succession and killed both men.

One of the other bandits came to stand by him. He looked at the fallen soldiers with a touch of horror in his eyes.

'Did you have to do that, Walt?' he asked bleakly.

'Sure, I had to do it. Unless you want them carryin' tales to the general,' the mean-faced one answered. 'I don't aim to have no soldier boys sayin' where they was bushwhacked and what we looked like. Tell 'em to kill the wounded and be quick about it. I want to get outa this place as soon as we can. It's a trap for us as well as for the bluebellies.'

His companions went about their killing without any more argument. They seemed to enjoy it and let out little whoops of delight as they fired at the wounded men. Only the bandit who had protested at the beginning, stood aside while the bodies were plundered for what little money they carried. He was older than the rest and now seemed to be regretting the whole thing.

Walt stood watching, his eyes alert and the shotgun reloaded as he waited for them to finish. They finally gathered round him again; seven of them – unwashed, unshaven, and covered in the dust of the trail. There were grins on some of their faces as they waited for more orders.

'We only want those last three wagons,' he told them brusquely. 'Move the others on to open ground and leave 'em there. Then get that dead horse unharnessed and another one put in its place. We gotta get the hell outa here fast as spit, and you two fellas can ride back of us and cover up the wagon tracks with branches.'

'Why not take all the wagons, Walt?' one of the men asked. 'Seems a shame to leave 'em here.'

The leader looked sourly at the questioner. 'We don't need 'em all,' he said angrily. 'The first four are full of food and beddin'. We got enough to eat and I don't aim to go around sellin' blankets. The stuff we need is in those three, and that's somethin' we can sell. Now, let's stop jawin' and get some work done. It's not safe to hang about this place.'

He stood watching as his companions carried out orders. The first four wagons contained light loads and had each been drawn by two horses. They moved rapidly from the confines of the small canyon as the animals went willingly for the new drivers. Once on open ground, the men unhitched the beasts and slapped their rumps to send them off to fend for themselves. Only one horse was retained to replace the animal that had been killed during the shooting. It was led back to the canyon and harnessed up.

Somebody unfastened the lashings on the canvas panels at the back of one of the remaining wagons and peered inside. He let out a gasp of astonishment. The others gathered round to take a look for themselves, while Walt moved over to stand behind them. He was grinning broadly, his bad teeth yellowish in the sallow face.

'Now, ain't you glad you came along for the ride?' he asked proudly. 'Did your Uncle Walt lead you to a real treasure or didn't he?'

'He sure as hell did,' one of the men said. 'You got friends in the right places, cousin.'

'Yah, and they don't even know they told me about this little collection. Drunken soldiers talk more than most, and I got me a nose for dollar bills. Now, you've seen enough, so get this lot outa here.'

While some of the men climbed on to the wagons, the rest hurried back along the canyon for their own horses that had been well hidden behind a group of stunted trees. The convoy drove out of the narrow trail into the open country, where the dust settled as the wheels of the wagons went across grass instead of the reddish earth of the canyon. They headed due west, with two of the horsemen bringing up the rear and dragging branches of trees behind their mounts to cover up the ruts made by the wheels. Once they were on deeper grass, the branches were discarded and the group travelled in a tighter formation; three men on the wagons, and the remaining five riding along the sides and pulling the spare horses behind them.

Walt drew level with the man driving the lead wagon. He reached out a hand to tap him on the knee.

'You remember the way, Bert?' he asked.

'Sure. I can find Methlin Creek with my eyes shut. We'll be there in a couple of hours if we keep up the pace. It all went off well, Walt. Your plannin' sure worked.'

His boss nodded and gestured the man to move over so that he could climb aboard the wagon and sit at his side. The man did as ordered and Walt tied the reins of his own mount to the rope securing the water barrel, and then edged himself from the saddle onto the wooden seat.

'You want the reins?' his companion asked.

'No, I just want a little family talk. Where we can't be overheard.'

The other man nodded. He was bigger and older

than Walt, with grey in his unshaven beard and pale eyes that watered as he drove.

'What're you figgerin'?' he asked suspiciously.

'Well, there's eight of us in this and some folk is goin' to get pretty impatient at havin' to wait for all the fuss to die down. They're goin' to want money to spend, and that can't be done until we're able to sell the stuff.'

'I reckon so, and when do we sell it?'

'Now, that's the trouble. The army is goin' to be real put-out at losin' three wagons so valuable, and havin' all them soldier boys killed. They're gonna turn out every goddam bluebelly in the area to hunt us down. So we gotta lay mighty low. No spendin', and no movin' about with a load of stolen army gear.'

The other man nodded. 'That figgers,' he agreed, 'but we took all the cash them soldiers was carryin', and you have a few dollars to pass around. It should last 'em a while.'

'It still don't amount to much, and you can't reckon on some of them bein' happy with a couple of drinks and a cheap whore when there's a fortune to be had. No, they're goin' to want that we should start tradin' right away. And that could be big trouble.'

'What are you goin' to do then, Walt? They ain't easy to argue with.'

'I was thinkin' of just keepin' it in the family. You take my drift?'

The man grinned. 'I sure do. The fewer around,

the bigger the share. A four-way split is better than eight ways. That how you reckon it?'

Walt looked carefully around to make sure that no other rider was within earshot.

'I was thinkin' more of three ways,' he murmured. 'Just you, me, and young Ed.'

'And cuttin' Cousin Will out of it as well?'

'Why not? He was chicken-livered back there. Let's just keep it close family, Bert.'

TWO

It took them nearly three hours to reach the canyon by Methlin Creek. It lay on the edge of a long, flat area that bore rank bushes dotted about amid tall grass that had wilted and yellowed in the sun. There was no sign of an entry to the place, but only a mass of cacti and mesquite. A rocky slope backed the greenery, darkly reddish in the fading light, and topped by a few ragged pines that seemed almost about to topple down onto the flat land below.

Walt signalled the men to halt while he donned a pair of old leather gloves and jumped down from the wagon. His brother tied the reins to the brake lever and joined him in front of the bushes.

While the others watched, the two men heaved the masses of prickly shrubs from the front of a trail that was clearly defined by an old dried-up water course. The cactus and mesquite plants had already been cut down and replanted in the soil so that they supported each other and looked like

permanent features to the casual eye. Their dead-
ness was hidden by the greying dust that had
blown about, so that they appeared little different
from the other masses of foliage that grew round
them.

Walt waved the wagons through and stood
admiring his own cleverness at the careful way he
had planned everything. It was the climax of a
lifetime of crime. He had pulled off the big one,
and only he and his two brothers were going to
share the wealth that was awaiting them.

When the little convoy was safely in the
canyon, Walt and his brother reblocked the
entrance again with the bushes, and carefully
wiped away any wheel ruts that had been left.
They then supervised the building of a fire so that
a meal could be made. The smell of coffee soon
filled the air while bacon sizzled in a skillet, and
beans heated to fill their empty bellies.

Walt gave his orders while they were eating.

'We're unloadin' the stuff here,' he told them,
'and hidin' it behind that line of trees. Then we
drive the wagons out the other end of the canyon
and go as far as the ridge along Manston way
where they used to dig for gold. We dump the
wagons there, turn the horses loose, and go about
our business like any other honest folk.'

One man stirred uneasily. He was large and fat,
with a round, dark face that bore a scar across one
pendulous cheek.

'What about sellin' the stuff?' he asked.

'Not yet. Like I just told Bert, the army is goin'
to be real busy. We gotta sell in Mexico and there's
no way we can get across the border until everything calms down. Now, I've got some money in
my poke and there's twenty dollars for each of
you. Spend it quiet and make it last. We come
back here in a few weeks and make the first
trade. I got friends down south waitin' for this
load, but it'll have to be in small lots.'

The fat man sucked his teeth and spat into the
fire.

'I don't like it,' he said. Some of the others
nodded surly agreement.

'You gotta like it, 'cos that's the way it's goin' to
be. This is big money and I planned everythin'
carefully. We're not goin' to bust the whole thing
wide open at this stage. You gotta have patience.'

'I got patience, sure enough, but I've three
dollars on me right now, and that with another
twenty ain't goin' to last very long.'

Walt was getting impatient. 'Then go rob some
old lady,' he snapped. 'We're all in the same corral,
and we gotta stay patient and outa trouble until
the right time. You knew the score before you
came into this, so don't start complainin' now.'

An older man stood up and threw away the
dregs of his coffee. He was grey-haired and
slightly stooped, and the younger ones looked at
him with a certain respect.

'I'll go along with that,' he said thoughtfully,
'but I do have a kinda problem, Walt?'

'What problem, Davy?'

'Well, I ain't aimin' to think ill of anyone, but let's face it, we're not the honestest bunch of choir boys you're like to meet at the church outin'.'

There was a little uneasy laughter, and even Walt managed a slight grin.

'What are you gettin' at, Davy?' he asked.

'Well, once we leave here, what's to stop somebody comin' back and movin' the stuff?'

There was a moment of silence as they all waited to see what their leader would say.

'That's a good point, Davy,' Walt grinned. 'I thought about it for a long time, and I reckon I got the answer fair and square. We all go to Tombstone together, and we stay there until it's time to come back here for the first load. If anyone should make a sudden journey, I don't figure as how the rest of us would look too kindly on him.'

'But what about money?' the fat man persisted. 'Tombstone's one expensive town.'

'We work.'

There was an even longer silence.

'I ain't worked in thirty years,' the fat man said angrily, 'and I don't aim to start now.'

Walt heaved a sigh. 'We do the sort of work we all know about,' he explained. 'There's a spread out near Rio Miranda run by an old widow woman and her two sons. They'll be easy pickings, so we can round up some of their cattle, take them a few miles north, and make ourselves a bit of money. By the time we've done that, maybe things will be quiet enough for us to start movin' this stuff.'

'Sounds fine to me,' Davy said. The others nodded agreement and even the fat man seemed happy.

'Right, let's unload the wagons, hide the stuff behind that mass of trees, and then make this place look as though nobody has been here.'

The men set to work, dragging down boxes of rifles, ammunition, dynamite, and saddlery. There were coils of fuse and several bundles of cavalry sabres to be shifted before they could reach a dozen barrels of gunpowder that everyone handled with exaggerated care. It all had to be carried across a small stream of fast-running water to the line of sycamores that grew like a screen along the walls of the canyon. A few willows rustled their branches in the gentle breeze and gave off showers of dust as the men brushed against them.

It was all over in an hour. The wagons were driven to the far end of the canyon where they waited while Walt and his brothers covered up their tracks and looked around for anything they had left lying near the camp site. Walt's youngest brother was tall and thin, with long hair bleached by the sun and the same mean face as the head of the family. He listened to his instructions and gave a wolfish grin when he heard what was proposed about sharing out the stolen army goods.

'When do we do it?' he asked eagerly.

'There's five of them and three of us,' Walt said carefully, 'so we gotta be sure to split them up. We'll keep together until we get rid of the wagons. Then I'll tell them that we go into Tombstone in three small groups. That'll make sense. Eight fellas ridin' into town as a bunch will be noticed – so we arrive there without any fuss. If I tell 'em that story, it'll be believed. You go in first, Ed, with fat Louis. We'll give you an hour start. When you're well out of earshot of us, kill them. Bert can ride in next with two of the others and do the same. I'll deal with Cousin Will and old Davy. Agreed?'

The other two nodded their heads.

Walt explained the plans to the rest of the gang as they drove the empty wagons towards the old mine workings. Everybody seemed quite happy with the arrangements and they reached their goal just as the sun was setting behind the long ridge of corroded sandstone.

'We could stay here for the night,' fat Louis suggested as they unhitched the draught horses.

Walt shook his head. 'Too risky. Them soldier boys will be lookin' for their wagons. All that stuff should have reached Fort Patterson by noon tomorrow. When they don't arrive, the army will start back-trailin'. I don't aim to be around when that happens. We'll lay up here another hour before settin' off north as arranged. You can all rest in Tombstone.'

He looked around the group. 'And don't go

makin' trouble there. They got law in that town.'

There was some slight laughter as they settled down around a hastily-built fire. The place was an arid spoil tip of different coloured earths, piled haphazardly by eager gold miners some six or seven years earlier. The wind was getting up, blowing the dust in little swirls and whistling through the few dried bushes that littered the ground.

One of the men was playing with a pistol, twirling it and repeatedly cocking it as he did so. Walt watched him carefully before walking slowly across and taking it from his surprised hand.

'Where in hell did you get this?' he asked angrily.

'From one of them soldier boys,' the man answered proudly. 'I reckon to give it a good home.'

Walt looked round the silent group. He waved the gun at them as if to emphasize the next move. Then he threw it as far as he could into a clump of bushes.

'I ain't takin' that from you, Walt!' the dispossessed one shouted. 'That gun's mine. Fair and square!'

He made a dive for the Colt at his belt and half drew it with his thumb on the hammer. Before it came fully into view, Walt pulled out his gun and fired a single shot. The man staggered for a moment before pitching forward with a light groan. They all watched as blood poured from the massive wound in his head.

'Did you have to do that, Walt?' Cousin Will asked.

'I did. If we want to stay alive through all this, we gotta act sensible-like. Think about it. That fool was goin' into Tombstone carryin' a soldier boy's gun. Those pieces have got numbers on them, and the military will be looking for strangers with stuff taken from that wagon train. We could have all hanged for that piece of scrap metal.'

They nodded reluctant agreement, eyeing him partly with admiration and partly with fear. Their leader took out his old watch and checked the time.

'We'd better start movin' along,' he said briskly. 'My brother Ed will go first with Louis. Head straight for Tombstone and put up at a cheap place. Don't make trouble, and don't get drunk. Use Ma Haggety's saloon so that we can all meet up there from time to time.'

'We'll need the money, Walt,' Ed reminded his brother.

'Sure.' The older man handed twenty dollars to each of them before watching the first two set off towards the north.

It was dark when the next pair set out. Bert only had one companion on the journey now. His other potential victim was already lying dead by the campfire. He caught Walt's eye as they parted

company, and the two brothers passed understanding glances.

Cousin Will went to the fire and poured out
some more coffee. He shivered in the growing cold
and kneeled miserably as close to the flames as he
could. Old Davy sat with his back to a rock,
placidly chewing tobacco and occasionally spitting
at whatever insect passed near enough. Walt was
restless.

He planned to wait for another hour or so and
then shoot them both while they were mounting
their horses. He would kill the old man first, and
then tackle his own cousin. He took out the
battered silver watch to look at it with the help of
the firelight. The moon was beginning to rise and
he would have no trouble keeping on the trail to
Tombstone. He felt the need of a strong drink, but
waited with growing impatience for the time to
pass.

It was about half an hour later that he heard the
noise. The other two men were dozing in front of
the built-up fire while Walt sat in the shadows
with his hands round the old tin mug that held
hot coffee.

He was not sure at first, but the horses pawed
the ground uneasily as he quietly drew his .44
and sat, unmoving, listening for the slight rattle
of gravel that had alerted him. Somebody was
creeping up on the camp.

Cousin Will stirred in his sleep and a piece of

wood fell from the fire, throwing some sparks into the cold air. The insects seemed louder as Walt sweated in spite of the chill. His eyes darted from shadow to shadow looking for an intruder. He at least had the consolation of knowing that he was in a dark corner of the camp. The gun was heavy in his hand as he waited.

A shotgun blast tore across the darkness and Cousin Will let out a yell of pain. Walt jumped to his feet and fired in the direction of the blast. Will was limping, his left leg a mass of blood as he pulled out his own gun and fired wildly.

'In those trees!' Walt shouted. He could see movement there. It was a big, fat man, and the firelight showed a livid scar across one cheek. Louis had come back, and that meant that brother Ed had been killed.

Walt cursed as he reloaded the Colt. Old Davy was shooting now, but not at Louis. There was a second man by the trees, using a Winchester as he fired from the hip. Old Davy reeled backwards as a bullet struck him in the left arm, but Walt noticed that the man with the carbine also staggered as the old fellow's pistol shot found a home.

There was total confusion now. Walt recognized the other man and there was despair in his face as he opened fire again. Louis and Ethan had obviously killed Walt's two brothers. They must have planned it from the beginning, and he felt outraged at their disloyalty. He tried to aim carefully in the flickering light and had the satisfaction of seeing Louis fall to his knees, still grasping the shotgun as he pitched forward.

Smoke was drifting across the scene. Ethan was on his knees too, still using the Winchester, while old Davy fired from a crouching position that seemed to indicate that he had received another wound. Cousin Will was on the ground, his gun in a bloody hand but still throwing lead in the direction of fat Louis. He fired back, although obviously wounded.

There were several more exchanges of shots as the horses fought their halters and the fire flung uneven shadows over the murderous scene.

Then it went all quiet and only one person was still alive, badly wounded and barely conscious.

Three

It was a small herd of cattle and only two men rode in the slow-moving wake of the animals. They were strays that were being gradually rounded up for the yearly trek to the nearest railroad. A pitiless sun beat down on the dry earth as the little group meandered slowly across the parched summer land.

The two cowpokes were getting on in years, both unshaven and poorly dressed, but one of them broad and solid in the saddle while the other was tall, gangling, and as thin as an undernourished steer. He had a long chin that moved rhythmically as he chewed tobacco.

His companion rode a little ahead as they topped a rise. He shaded his eyes with a gnarled hand and peered at the shimmering horizon for any more strays. There was a rocky outcrop in the far distance, with a mass of stunted bushes growing to waist height below the reddish walls. The men urged the animals forward, not hurrying

25

them too much as the steers cropped what sweet grass was left along the way.

It was the broad man who spotted the trampled ground with its mass of hoof marks that seemed to disappear into the clumps of bushes at the bottom of the cliff. The vegetation had been uprooted and crushed as cattle passed through the tangle of undergrowth to get closer to the wall of fissured rock.

The rider stopped his horse and waited for his companion to join him. He pointed out the marks to the thin man and both of them noticed the sudden liveliness among their own animals. Even their well-managed horses were raising their heads and looking towards the line of reddish stone.

'There's water back there,' the broad man said, 'and I reckon we've gotten ourselves a few more strays.'

The other man nodded and set his own horse on the trail of crushed bushes. It went down a slope that gradually led round an angle in the rock formation and broadened the trail into a shady canyon, its confines littered with willow and stunted sycamores. There were several steers ahead, browsing quietly among the taller grass that was still green and sweet from a small, shallow stream that ran down the centre of what was really a little oasis in the dried-out summer heat. One of the steers looked at the intruders before going back to eating its fill.

The horsemen were followed into the canyon by

the rest of the cattle. The animals headed straight for the water and lapped thirstily while the two riders let their own mounts drink and splash their hooves while they surveyed the scene.

'I reckon there's five of our brand in here,' the thin man said cheerfully, 'and them other eight is from Ned Tyrer's place. He'll be glad to get 'em back. He ain't so flush for marketable steers this season.'

The broad man nodded. He got down from his horse and stretched luxuriously.

'We may as well have a rest here,' he said. 'I could surely use a cup of coffee and somethin' to eat. How about it?'

'As good a place as we'll find, and the cattle won't go strayin' from that water.'

The broad man started collecting wood for a fire while his companion loosened the cinches on the horses and began unpacking the saddle-bags. He suddenly stopped what he was doing and looked carefully at the ground. The animals had churned up the earth to disclose a scattering of black ashes.

'Hey, Jake!' he called. 'Somebody's been here before us. There's ashes from a fire.'

'It don't mean nothin'. We ain't the first in the world to light on this place.'

The broad man came back down the draw with a bundle of kindling in his arms. He looked at where his colleague was pointing and kicked the ashes with his boot.

'Seems to be pretty old, Jethro,' he murmured,

'but why did they cover them up?'

'That's what I wondered on. Rustlers?'

'Could be, and all them bushes at the mouth of this canyon was all pulled up and then put back to hide the entrance. They could have kept steers here after raidin' somebody's spread.'

'Ain't heard of no rustlin' round here lately.'

'No.'

Jake Cotter shrugged his shoulders and began building the fire. They ate a meal, drank plenty of hot coffee, and took a long rest while the heat of the day passed. The only noises were of grazing cattle and the steady hum of insects.

When it was time to go, the two men mounted up and began checking their small herd. They gradually got them all together and headed out of the canyon, well fed and watered. Jake was counting the steers as they emerged onto the open land again.

'How many did you spot in there?' he asked his partner.

'Thirteen. Five with our brand and eight from the Tyrer spread.'

'Then we're one short. I reckon as how it's behind that row of trees back there. Hold 'em while I ride over and flush it out.'

Jake swung his cow pony across the little stream, and pushed through a gap in the closely-packed trees that formed a row as straight as a line of soldiers near the canyon wall. A solitary steer turned its dull gaze on him as he appeared among the tall grass that grew in tufts along the base of the rocks. He began to manoeuvre the animal back towards the herd when he saw something half-buried among the foliage. He pulled at the reins and looked down at the dust-covered crate that was almost hidden by leaves and gravel. Jake got down from the horse and, steers forgotten, bent down to examine his find.

He pulled aside some of the other bushes and discovered more heavy wooden crates. They bore stencilled numbers on their sides and the lids were firmly nailed down. He called to Jethro while hunting around behind the screen of sycamores. There were more boxes there, buried among the foliage and dust of the canyon. There were also saddles – several dozen of them with sets of harness tied to each pommel.

'What in hell's keepin' you, fella?' Jethro shouted as he appeared between the trees.

'I found us somethin' real important,' Jake grinned. 'Look at this lot for a heap of treasure.'

The other man joined him in front of one of the crates and took out a knife to prise open the lid. The blade snapped but they were able to break off two of the panels to disclose the contents.

'Well, fry me for a mule-skinner!' Jethro exclaimed as he stared at the neatly packed rifles. 'This sure beats first prize in a turkey shoot. How did they get here, Jake?'

His partner pondered on the matter for a few moments.

'Remember about four, five months ago?' he mused. 'The army lost three wagons down in Fresco Canyon. All them soldier boys got themselves killed and the stuff was never found. Well, I reckon we just lighted on it. The biggest heap of guns, dynamite, ammunition and saddles you ever did see outside a fort.'

Jethro kicked another crate and broke into a wide grin.

'I reckon there could be a good reward for this lot,' he said slowly. 'The bluebellies would be mighty glad to get it back.'

Jake Cotter nodded absent-mindedly. He was moving among the boxes, counting them and frowning as he thought out the situation.

'There's a thousand dollars reward,' he said after a while. 'That's five hundred each.'

Jethro whistled. 'That's more than we earn in a year,' he murmured. 'I'd sure like to get my hands on that sort of money, Jake. Why do you reckon the stuff has been left here?'

'Well, as I heard tell about it, them bandits just rode off with the valuable wagons and then their bodies were found a couple of weeks later up near Manston way. They seemed to have had a shoot-out over it. That's how the County Sheriff figured things out. They must have dumped it here first, but now they ain't never comin' back for the stuff. It's all ours, Jethro. And worth not a cent under twenty thousand dollars, so the rumours go.'

The thin man's eyes narrowed at the words. He

looked slyly at his colleague.

'You figurin' on somethin', Jake?' he asked quietly.

'Well, we ain't exactly young any more, and this sorta life don't make for old bones. I always fancied a small spread with a few cattle, a nice fishin' creek, and a coupla hands to do the real work. What do you want for your old age?'

Jethro shrugged. 'Ain't really thought about it,' he admitted, 'but I once passed a gun store in Tombstone. Real smart place it was. I like guns – the feel of them, the looks. Maybe I'd open me a gun store. Get some clean clothes. Stay indoors when the weather was actin' up. Yeah, I reckon that'd do me.'

'Well, five hundred dollars each wouldn't run to that. But a few thousand each. . . !'

'Could we do it, Jake?' The voice was eager but scared.

Jake sat down on one of the boxes and kicked sand with his worn boot.

'As I see it,' he said softly, 'the fellas who stole all this had planned everythin' careful-like. They figured on leavin' the stuff here until the army got tired of lookin' for it. Then they was goin' to move it out. Probably a bit at a time. Havin' a fight over it spoiled all their nice little plans, so it's still here and they're likely to be all dead. A fella told me that the Tombstone newspapers say they killed each other. Maybe, maybe not.'

'If any of them is alive, they'll be back here.'

'Well, they ain't turned up yet, so I reckon we got a chance. What we have to do is to get these cattle back, finish our time goin' to the railhead, and then collect our pay and hire a wagon. We move this lot to a new place, so that if any of them are alive, it just ain't here no more.'

'Suppose they come back before we do?'

Jake shrugged. 'Can't be helped. But it's been here for months, so we gotta hope it'll still be here when we bring the wagon.'

'And where will we move it to?'

'I bin figurin' on that. There's a line of mine shafts along the Nepa Valley. They're all worked out and nobody goes there no more. The water's bad and the cattle keep clear of it. We'll hide the stuff at the back of one of the tunnels and move it out a bit at a time. Nothin' too much or it'll draw attention to us.'

'Yeah, but who's goin' to buy?'

Jake grinned. 'Same folk as I reckon they was plannin' to sell to. Mexicans.'

'Will they have that sort of cash?'

'I figure. We'll make a few enquiries around Nogales. I got one or two friends there, and they know what goes on across the border. Them Mexican fellas is always buyin' guns for some revolution or other.'

'Why not sell to our own folk? There's a lot of money up north.'

'Too risky. Everythin' will have an army mark on it, and all the lawmen will still be lookin' hard so that they can collect the reward. No, Jethro, I reckon that you and me is goin' into the sellin' business in a big way.'

Four

Jake Cotter was carrying a heavy sack of flour as he left the store. His two large hands grasped the bag to his broad chest and his red face was flushed even more by the exertion. He walked across the boardwalk and down the two wooden steps to his wagon. It was just then that somebody fired a shot.

It was a startling noise in the peaceful dullness of a small Arizona town. The few people on the main street stopped in their tracks. They looked anxiously about while some of the women cowered in the shelter of the nearest building. A buzzard flew noisily up from the church roof.

In the following silence, Jake could hear a persistent little sound that was like the dripping of water. He looked down and saw a small pile of flour gathering at his feet. There was a bullet hole in the sack, and the shot had been meant for him.

He tipped his burden onto the wagon before

looking across the street from where the shot must have come. There was a saloon there, its swing doors motionless and nobody in sight. Jake Cotter checked the old Colt .44 at his belt, took a shotgun from the wagon, and started to cross the street with determined strides.

Out of the corner of his eye he could see Marshal Brad Stone hurrying from the jailhouse. He was also carrying a shotgun and his hat blew off as he ran as fast as his short, thin legs would carry him, Marshal Stone was getting on in years. He had a quiet town and liked it that way. The days of gold mining were over and Elinor township was now a faded place that relied on the surrounding farms and timber businesses to keep it alive. He came up to Jake Cotter, stopping him in his tracks.

'Who fired that shot?' he asked in a high, thin voice. 'Was it you, Jake?'

'No, it was fired *at* me. Hit the sack of flour I was loadin' on the wagon. I reckon it came from over there.'

Jake Cotter nodded towards the Golden Eagle saloon. The marshal's eyes followed his gesture.

'And you was on your way to find out who did it?' he asked.

'I figure to do just that. If a fella can't come into town for a few supplies, then there's somethin' wrong.'

The marshal pulled a face. 'You ain't the most popular visitor in these parts, Jake,' he said bleakly. 'Folks is all against you these days. They don't reckon as how you've played fair with them.'

'Is that how you feel, Brad?'

The marshal shook his head. 'Not really, but I'm the fella what's caught in the middle of all this. If folks go gunnin' for you, I must try and keep the peace. It's my town and I have a duty. But these folk are decent and law-abidin'. They think they got real cause to dislike you. My advice is to load up your wagon and go. I'll stand guard while you do it.'

Jake Cotter stood undecided for a moment. He was a stubborn man with a determined set to his features, and his firm mouth bore more than a hint of suppressed violence.

'Somebody shot at me,' he said grimly, 'and I don't aim to take that sort of treatment. I've lived round here all my life, just like you have, and I ain't figurin' on bein' driven out by a cowardly gunslinger that you're too scared to tackle. Now, get outa my way, Brad, and let me do the job you should be doing.'

The marshal flushed angrily but lowered the shotgun.

'Have it your way, Jake,' he muttered, 'but if you get into trouble back there, I ain't goin' to be around for you.'

'I ain't relyin' on you, Brad. Never did, and never will do. If they scare me outa Elinor township, where in hell would I get my supplies? Next decent store is thirty miles south. I gotta stand up to them.'

The marshal nodded and turned on his heel. He picked up his hat as he walked slowly back to the jailhouse under the stares of a gradually increasing crowd of people, who looked on in silence with neutral expressions on their faces. They stepped aside as Jake Cotter completed his walk across the dusty street and entered the saloon.

It was quite dim inside, smelling of stale beer and food, and with only three customers at that time of day. They all leaned on the bar, close together, talking as though they had heard nothing of the shooting. The bartender was at the far end of the counter, washing glasses and trying to look as if he was not there.

The drinkers did not even turn round when Jake Cotter let the doors swing behind him and began crossing the floor to where they drank. It was the clicking of the shotgun hammers that finally brought them to life. They put down their glasses to turn with fear on their faces.

Jake recognized two of them. They were men of his own age – miners who had panned gold on the Gila River and spent the money on gambling and drink over the years. They were unshaven now, with old clothes and an aura of no hope around them. The third man was younger, with a mean, thin face and dark eyes that never seemed to keep still. He already had a hand near the holster at his side, and it was at him that Jake levelled the gun.

'You go for that, fella,' he said flatly, 'and I'll spread you all over the floor.'

The man seemed about to say something but changed his mind. His right hand moved gently away from the butt of the pistol and Jake noticed that it was a damaged hand, scarred and reddened by a recent wound. It was one of the older men who spoke.

'What's got into you, Jake?' he asked with a grin. 'You seem kinda jumpy.'

'Yeah, it's the way I get when somebody takes a shot at me.'

The man grinned again, a little nervously. 'I thought we heard a noise out there,' he said, 'but we ain't the pushy types. We was just takin' a quiet drink and mindin' our own business.'

'I'm glad to hear that. I reckon that means that none of you has fired a gun in the last few minutes.'

The three men shrugged while the bartender reached below the counter. Jake Cotter swung the shotgun around.

'If you're thinkin' of doin' somethin', fella,' Jake said tautly, 'you could just end up as the dumbest corpse in town.'

The man licked his lips and showed both hands above the counter.

'I ain't lookin' for trouble, Mr Cotter,' he pleaded, 'but the boss don't want no disturbance in here.'

'I noticed he wasn't around,' Jake said as he glanced towards the stairs. 'Now, suppose we find out who's been shootin' at folks this morning.' He motioned at the three drinkers with the barrel of the shotgun. 'Just take out your pistols carefullike and put 'em on the bar top. Then back against the wall, and don't do anythin' that might upset me.'

'Now, look here, Cotter . . . !' one of the men began. The shotgun waved again and he decided not to argue. The three Colts were laid on the counter and their owners backed off against the wall near an empty card table. Jake picked up the guns one by one and sniffed the barrels. None of them had been fired or contained empty shell cases.

'Maybe the shot came from some place else,' one of the men suggested.

'You reckon so, Harry?'

Jake looked at the four glasses on the bar top as the man nodded dumbly.

'There's somebody missing,' he said, 'and they ain't slipped out the back door, 'cos as I remember this place, it ain't got a back door.'

He looked round the saloon as the men watched anxiously.

'I was havin' a drink with them,' the bartender said helpfully.

'Were you, now? I'll remember you said that, fella.'

Jake picked up the guns from the bar top, putting his fingers through the trigger guards and still keeping the shotgun levelled at the inhabitants of the saloon. He backed towards the door and flung the weapons into the street. He knew that the gunman could either have gone up the stairs or was in the back room, waiting for a chance to leave. He could even have been hiding behind the counter and Jake knew that his own position was a dangerous one. He backed out onto the boardwalk and stood irresolutely for a moment.

The people on the street looked at him without sympathy. He could see the marshal up near the jailhouse, and at the other end of the street the preacherman was striding purposefully from his white wooden church. The last thing Jake Cotter wanted at that moment was the fluttering nonsense of the clergy.

He hurried round the corner of the saloon, and as he had half suspected, the rear window was raised and there was a mess of fresh footprints in the dust beneath it. The man who had shot at him was well gone. He cursed and went back to his wagon where the patient horses looked on with a total lack of interest. The storekeeper had piled the rest of his goods outside the door. It was a strong hint that he need not enter the building again. Jake loaded the supplies onto the wagon and looked around the street once more.

Nobody came out of the saloon to claim the guns, and none of the passing townsfolk bothered to pick them up.

Jake climbed aboard, took the reins in his large hands, and gave them a shake across the backs of the sturdy animals. The preacher reached him just as the rig was pulling away. Jake Cotter cursed under his breath and pulled at the reins. The Reverend Daniel Bride was a tall man with longish grey hair and a pale face under his broad black hat. His skinny wrists stuck out from beneath the sleeves of the long frock coat, and he laid one hairy hand on the flank of a horse to stroke it.

'Don't go rushing off now, Jake,' he admonished with what passed for a smile with him. It was merely the opening of a mournful mouth to disclose a row of large, yellowish teeth. The rest of his gaunt face remained dour and disapproving of a sinful world.

'I ain't welcome in my own home town no more, Preacher,' Jake said impatiently. 'If you go talkin' to me, somebody round here might just take a shot at you as well. It ain't worth the risk.'

'Jake, my dear old friend, this has gone on long enough. Come round and take a cup of coffee with me. My wife has just made it. You could stay for a meal too. We've plenty to spare and you'll surely recall what a cook she is.'

The voice was rich and gravelly – the voice of a man used to speaking to an audience.

'Well, Reverend. I don't really. . . .'

'We need to talk, Jake. This has to stop.'

The preacher's voice was urgent and Jake Cotter nodded a reluctant agreement.

'I'll come along,' he said quietly, 'but there ain't

nothin' I can do about all this trouble. I never done nobody harm in my life, but I'm sure gettin' mad as hell at the folks round here who treat me as bad as they'd treat a bunch of horse-thieves.'

He set the horses in motion while the preacher walked alongside the wagon. His long strides kept up easily as they went down the main street and cut through a side lane to the white-washed wooden church with the preacher's modest clapboard house beside it. There was a neat little garden with a stable and privy to the rear. The house had a peaceful look and the smell of the garden plants wafted on the air as Jake halted the rig and climbed down to join the Reverend Bride.

The two men marched up the path: one tall and gangling; the other short, stocky, and carrying his shotgun in the crook of a muscled arm.

Mrs Bride was a stout and jolly woman, the opposite to her dour husband, and she made Jake Cotter welcome as an old friend and schoolmate. They sat down to the fragrant coffee while the afternoon sun lit up the well-furnished room with its polished harmonium against one wall, lines of leather-bound volumes set neatly in a large oak cabinet, and fresh antimacassars on each chair.

'You must expect people to be angry, Jake,' Reverend Bride said as he supped noisily from his large cup. 'You was poor once and you must know how they feel. You're one rich man all of a sudden, and it happens just when the gold sites have been worked out. Folk think that you've found a new claim and you're keeping it to yourself. It's jealousy, Jake. That's what human beings is about. They envy you your good luck.'

Jake Cotter picked up a sweet biscuit and finished it in one large bite. He had eaten nothing since leaving home and could smell cooking in the Brides' kitchen.

'Look, Reverend,' he said firmly, 'I got no gold mine to share. I have a little business deal goin', and I need to leave home every now and then to collect some cash that's owin' me. It's a few days journey each way and that's why I stock up like some prospector. But there ain't no gold. Never was.'

The preacher shook his head sadly. 'Jake,' he said, 'you brought dust and nuggets back to town on more than one occasion. Words gets round in a small place like this, and Elijah Little is not the tightest-lipped banker in the world. He told the mayor, the mayor's wife spread it around, and the whole town is talking of a new gold strike. There has to be a better explanation than that to convince them.'

He waited patiently for the other man to say something. All that Jake Cotter did was to stand up, wipe his mouth, and offer a handshake.

'I won't wait for a meal, Reverend,' he said quietly. 'It's best if I head off home before another gun-happy fella tries to shoot me. I don't want to involve you and your good lady, so just give her my thanks and believe me when I say there ain't no gold.'

The preacher stood up and took the proffered hand.

'They won't accept that, Jake,' he said sadly. 'Folks is set on the idea that you are letting your friends down by keeping it all a secret. They reckon that there's enough for all and that you owe them something.'

'I owe them nothing, Reverend. What I have, I worked for. When they was all scramblin' around up Tombstone way and along the Gila River, I was workin' cattle for a few dollars a week. They came back to Elinor with more money than I could ever hope for. And what did most of 'em do? They spent it in Ma Roger's place or in the saloons. Only Ed Naylor and Frank Wilde had sense enough to buy businesses and land. Nobody gave me a grub-stake or asked me how I was fixed for a few dollars.'

The preacher nodded silent agreement as Jake paused for an angry breath.

'And I had a sick wife in them days. You was the only one who helped. You and your good lady. But not the rest of this town. And now that I've hit on a deal that brings me in an income a couple of times a year, they all get jealous. Sure, I had gold once or twice. That was because my customers paid me that way. But I ain't found a mine or a river full of nuggets or dust. So, tell 'em that. And tell 'em that if anybody else tries to shoot me, I'll be shootin' back.'

His voice rose as he spoke and the preacher spread his arms despairingly.

'They won't believe it. At least give me something real to tell them, Jake,' he pleaded. 'It's the only way to stop this.'

Jake Cotter picked up his shotgun and opened the front door. He hesitated for a moment before answering.

'Well, I can tell you this much, Reverend,' he said slowly. 'This ain't just my secret. I got a partner to consider, and I don't reckon on him likin' his affairs bein' talked over in Elinor township. I ain't exactly proud of the business we're in, but it's no concern of other folk. We ain't doin' no harm and we just want to be let alone to go our ways.'

He nodded his farewell and went out to the stoop. The sun was hot now with a faint breeze that blew little ripples of dust around the hoofs of the patient horses. Jake unhitched their nosebags and was just about to mount the wagon when the shot rang out.

Five

The horses reared and moved the wagon forward a few yards. It was the preacher who grabbed for the reins while Jake Cotter levelled the shotgun as he looked around to see who had done the shooting. A solitary bird flew up from the garden, and after a few dizzying turns, alighted on a fence post.

At the junction of the main street and the path that led to the preacher's house, a single figure stood swaying in the bright sunlight. He was an elderly man, short and stooped, with an unshaven face and lank grey hair that protruded from the old felt hat with its sweaty band and faded Union Army badge. He held a Colt .44 in his right hand and advanced on Jake Cotter despite the steady barrels of the shotgun.

The preacher rushed forward, his large hands outstretched in supplication.

'Don't do it, Steve!' he shouted. 'Jake'll kill you

sure as spit. Just settle this quietly like Christian folk.'

The old man halted in his tracks as the clergyman stood firmly between him and his target.

'Keep outa this, Reverend,' he slurred. 'Me and Jake has things to settle. Move aside.'

Jake Cotter levelled the shotgun, edging round the preacher as he did so.

'Drop it, Steve!' he bawled. 'Or I'll do exactly what the Reverend Bride said I would. I got no quarrel with any man, but I don't aim to have folk shootin' at me. Drop the gun or you're one dead man.'

The Colt wavered uncertainly in the old fellow's hand, and it was while he was still undecided that the marshal came round the corner. He calmly took the gun from him and shoved it into his own belt while at the same time grabbing the old man by the arm to escort him slowly down the main street to the jailhouse. Jake Cotter lowered the shotgun while Preacher Bride settled his starched linen cuffs beneath the edge of his black sleeves.

'I gotta thank you for steppin' out there, Reverend,' Jake said with a grin. 'He could have killed either of us.'

'He is a poor, deluded fool, Jake, but you can see how feelings are in Elinor. People are jealous of your wealth. They think you've discovered a mine or a river where there's gold. And they want their share.'

Jake Cotter smiled bitterly. 'If there was such a

place, I'd be a fool to share the secret, Reverend,' he said.

'Jake, you can remember the last rush. You were punching cattle for old man Duncan at the time, and all of a sudden there was a chance for you to make a fortune. All your neighbours were up on the Gila River, sharing out their claims. They worked together, not begrudging the better luck of some, and the discouragement of others. Is it any wonder that they feel you're letting them down?'

Jake nodded. 'I see your point, but there ain't no gold.'

'Jake, you won't convince them.' The preacher's voice was urgent. 'You didn't take part in the rush for gold. You stayed out on the range, earning a pittance and supporting your family. Then all of a sudden, when the mines were worked out, you bought the old Lannigan place, came into town, and put a hefty sum of money into the bank. You bought store furniture, a new wagon, and some real good animals. It's not surprising that folk started jumping to conclusions.'

Jake Cotter gathered up the reins of the horses and climbed aboard his rig.

'I'll tell you this for the last time, Preacher,' he said grimly, 'I never found no gold and I ain't beholden to nobody in this town. Sure, I'm rich, because I done me some good tradin'.'

'Not from selling your cattle, Jake Cotter,' the preacher said sharply. 'You ain't got enough steers to be worth even a thousand dollars, and you sure haven't got timber enough to turn into a fortune. You spend your time fishing the creek and lolling about on your porch. That's what folks say.'

Jake grinned. 'And they're sayin' right,' he admitted. 'I don't aim to work no more than I have to. Old Abraham and young Davy can run my small spread while I take it nice and easy like some well-heeled city gentleman. And there ain't no harm in that. The Lord knows I worked hard all my days.'

Parson Bride frowned his disapproval. 'That may well be, Jake, but you have to admit that twice a year, you come into town, load up on supplies and then vanish for a few weeks. And when you come back, you got more money to pay into the bank.'

Jake smiled again. 'That money-lendin' fella sure gabs,' he chuckled. 'If there was another bank in town, I'd give them my business. So I goes on a trip twice a year. What's it to anybody? I mind my business, and I just ask that they mind theirs.'

He whipped up the horses and the heavy wagon moved off to head out of town towards the south. The preacher watched the departure with a slow shake of his grizzled head. As he turned towards the house again, two figures appeared from the main street. He stopped to wait for them.

Banker Little and the marshal were side by side, their eyes following the disappearing wagon.

Elijah Little was a youngish man to be the manager of a bank. He was tall, well built, but already running to fat. His pale face was smooth and round, with a ragged moustache that curled slightly at the edges. He was panting with the exertion of having hurried from his office to see what was going on. The marshal was calmer. He had left Steve Welling behind bars and had hoped for a word with Jake Cotter before the rancher left town. The two men joined the preacher and looked at each other with worried expressions.

'Does he still say there's no gold?' the marshal asked.

Parson Bride nodded glumly. 'He does. Insists that it's all down to business deals.'

'He brought dust into the bank on two occasions,' Elijah Little gasped. 'Twenty ounces at one time, and nearly forty ounces the following year. Then there were those nuggets I told you about. Real beauties they were. Absolutely pure. No wonder the town's feeling sore about it.'

The marshal shook his head sadly. 'I warned him,' he said. 'Being shot at by an old drunk like Steve is one thing, but there are other folks here who might not miss if they decide to start usin' guns. We're a community, and Jake Cotter's not behavin' in a neighbour-like way. He's gotta come clean with folk and give everyone a chance. If he registers a claim, he'll leave the rest of the area free to others. It ain't askin' too much, and it sure as hell would make things more peaceful round here.'

'It would be good business too,' the banker said eagerly. 'Remember what Elinor was like when they were all panning the Gila River or digging near Tombstone?'

Marshal Stone nodded at the fond remembrance. 'I had two deputies then,' he said. 'The saloons were open nearly all night. Ma's place was lit up like a Fourth of July celebration, and the stores were packed with fancy big-town goods. We're just a backwater place now. And like to remain so.'

Although the preacher had frowned at the mention of saloons and bawdy houses, he had to admit that people gave generously to church funds during the gold-rush days.

'I tried to talk sense into him,' he said. 'Tried to point out his Christian duty, but Jake Cotter's a man who's surely bent on getting himself into trouble.'

'What are you going to do with old Steve Welling?' the banker asked the lawman.

Marshal Stone shrugged. 'I'll let him go when Cotter's well clear of town. There's no harm in the old fella, but when he's had a few drinks and sees Jake loadin' up his wagon with all the best goods, he does get a bit excited. They were friends once, so I reckon he feels that Jake owes him.'

He drew the other two men nearer to him. 'It ain't Steve I'm worried about,' he said in a low voice. 'There's another fella in town with as mean a face as you could wish to see. He was proppin' up the bar of the Golden Eagle and talkin' to Steve and a couple of other old-timers. From what I can get out of the old man, this stranger was buyin' drinks and askin' questions about Jake Cotter. He might even have set Steve Welling on to takin' a shot at him.'

'And you've no idea who he is?' the preacher asked.

'No, but he's one real mean fella, and unless he starts somethin', I don't aim to make his acquaintance. He looks like he's seen plenty of trouble. Got hisself a limp and a damaged hand.'

The other two men saw his point of view and they walked slowly up the corner of the main street to see if Jake Cotter's wagon was still in sight. There was a lingering haze of dust in the air but the man was far from the town and on his way back to the ranch.

'I figure I can let Steve out of the jailhouse now,' the marshal said with a grin. 'He ain't got nothin' but a mule so I reckon on him coolin' down some and sleepin' it off. He sure won't go out to Jake's place now that I've taken his gun away.'

'Drink is a bad councillor to a disappointed man,' the preacher said piously. 'Steve Welling would be the better for getting to his knees and praising the Lord.'

'He ain't got much to praise him for,' Brad Stone said bluntly. 'The Lord didn't do much for him when his wife died or when his son was killed in the war. No wonder he took to drink.'

'He lacked faith,' the preacher snapped as he turned away to stalk back towards his house. The other two men grinned and began to walk down the main street.

'I hope Jake stays away from town,' the marshal said as they neared the bank.

Elijah looked a little doubtful. 'He spends money in Elinor,' he said doggedly, 'and he's a good customer of mine. We could do with more like him.'

'Not if it leads to shootings.'

'Do you think he really has a mine?'

Marshal Stone paused in his stride. They were now opposite the store where the shooting had taken place. He looked across at the saloon before answering.

'You was the one who began all this, Elijah,' he said quietly. 'You went gossipin' about the money he was payin' in, and told all about the gold dust and nuggets. Word got around, and folks began talkin' of a mine. That started all the trouble.'

The banker flushed angrily. 'I did no such thing!' he protested. 'Everybody could see the way his life suddenly changed. He bought that spread, hired a couple of hands, and made it obvious that he had cash to burn. I only mentioned to my wife and one or two of the folks in business that he was bringing a bit of prosperity to Elinor township.'

'You went on like a real windbelly. It was talk of the gold what did it. Mention gold and the folks round here get the urge to go prospectin' again.'

While the marshal was talking, he was watching a man emerge from the Golden Eagle saloon. It was the mean-looking stranger who had been at the bar with some of the elderly locals. The man limped to his horse, tightened the girth, and without a glance at the two men, rode out of town. He was going in the same direction as that taken by Jake Cotter.

Marshal Stone bit his lip uneasily. He felt a need to have another talk with Steve Welling.

Six

The old drunk was sitting on the cot in the only cell that was still in use. The other two had been employed as storage for the contents of the marshal's home when he moved out after the death of his wife. He lived now in the back room of the jailhouse and was waiting impatiently for the day when he could retire to go and live with his eldest son near Tucson. He just needed a little extra money, like most other folks, and a gold find was the only way of getting it.

He unlocked the cell and beckoned Steve Welling out. There was coffee on the stove and he poured out a couple of mugs and passed one across to the prisoner. They both sat down on opposite sides of the large desk.

'Well, Steve, you sure as hell got yo'self into trouble back there,' the lawman said with an official frown. 'What started it all?'

'I took a few drinks too many, Marshal,' the old man said contritely. 'You know how it is. You gets talkin' with a few old friends, and things come up in the conversation.'

'Like Jake Cotter and his gold mine?'

'Yeah.' The man nodded eagerly. 'There we was, just jawin' about him, when his wagon pulls into town with him all perky and well-fed. I got kinda mad. We was friends in the old days, and I reckon he owes me. He owes all the town. If there's gold around here, I figure as how we all need a chance to work it. It just ain't neighbourly to keep it a secret. A fella could get hisself killed that way.'

'Yeah, he nearly did get hisself killed, Steve. You sure tried hard enough out there.'

'Hell, Marshal. You know me better than that,' the old man chortled. 'When have I ever missed anythin' I aimed at? My eyes ain't what they was, but I can still shoot as straight as the next fella.'

Brad Stone thought it over. 'That's true enough, Steve,' he admitted, 'but you had been drinkin' with those friends of yours. Tell me, who was that fella with the mean face and a limp? Seemed a stranger to me.'

'Stranger to all of us, but he bought the drinks fair enough.'

'Why?'

The old man blinked as he thought about it. 'Well, I reckon he wanted information,' he conceded. 'Sure was one nosy fella – like I told you earlier.'

The marshal's voice was silky. 'What exactly did he want to know?' he asked.

Steve held out the mug for more coffee and the lawman poured some out for both of them. He waited patiently.

'Well, he was real interested in any local folk what had gotten rich in the last two years or so. Said he'd heard that some local fella had struck lucky one way or another.'

'And you told him about Jake Cotter?'

The old fellow shifted uneasily in his chair. 'I might have mentioned it,' he admitted, 'but Fred and old Ely put in their two cents' worth as well. Jake's name did come up when we was talkin', and then, bust me if he don't appear across the street at the store.'

'And this stranger suggested it might be a good idea if you took a shot at him?'

'Hell, no. He tried to stop me, Marshal. But I was all fired-up by that time and I figured to scare the hell outa Jake. You know what a few drinks does to you.'

The lawman nodded. 'I know what they do to you,' he said. 'So you fired a shot across the street and then legged it out the side window. Is that right?'

'Just about. I saw Jake comin' across with a shotgun, and he looked like he was loaded for bear. I didn't wait around for trouble, Marshal. I just got the hell outa there.'

'Tell me about this stranger. What name did he hand out?'

Steve Welling shook his head slowly. 'I don't

recollect him sayin' what he was called,' he admitted. 'He just said he was passin' through and was tryin' to find a man who'd cheated him outa money a few years back. That's why he was askin' after anybody who'd gotten rich, sudden-like.'

'Did he say what he'd do if he caught up with the fella?'

The old man laughed. 'No siree, but I reckon there weren't a lot he could do. His gun hand was bad hurt and he limped like a three-legged mule. Been in a real fight some time, he had.'

'Had he now?' The marshal stroked the side of his face thoughtfully. 'Tell me, Steve, have you thought about what would happen if Jake Cotter did get himself killed? Asides from hangin' you, that is.'

'Well . . . I only aimed to scare him. . . .'

'Yeah, so you say. But if somebody killed Jake, this town would have no chance of findin' that mine of his. We gotta keep him alive, fella. Without Jake Cotter, none of us can get rich. You follow me?'

Steve Welling blinked rapidly. 'Yeah, I reckon as how you have the right of it there, Marshal,' he said slowly.

'So the best way of discoverin' the gold would be to keep a watch on him. He's just been into town for stores. So that means that he's off again very soon. If you was to follow. . . !'

He waited for the words to sink in and was

pleased to see the old man's face light up. Then it fell again.

'That'd mean gettin' supplies and a horse, Marshal,' he said sadly. 'I ain't got neither. Only my old mule, and she moves real slow these days.'

'Somebody might stake you. If you was in partnership.'

Steve Welling thought about it for a moment, looking slyly at the lawman in case it was some sort of trap.

'Who?' he asked.

'I've got a couple of mules in the corral that are eatin' their heads off. Ten dollars would buy an awful lotta food. You got your own gun, so I reckon you'd be as well equipped as any other fella for a little trailin' job.'

Steve Welling sat motionless. He was weighing up the chance that he was being offered the way to a possible fortune. His tongue was moistening dry lips as he clutched the coffee mug tightly in anxious hands.

'Is we goin' to be partners, Marshal?' he asked tentatively.

'Why not? I can't leave town for weeks on end, but you can. After all, you are a prospector, and you never can tell, Steve, Jake Cotter might lead you straight to a gold mine.'

'Would – er – the whole town have to know?'

The marshal grinned. 'I thought that was what you wanted?'

'Oh, sure. But I figure we should stake our

claim first. Seems only right.'

'I can't argue with that. And there is one other thing. Nothin' must happen to Jake. We'll never hit on the mine without him. So just make sure that nobody goes gunnin' for him. And I'm thinkin' of that mean-faced coyote in particular.'

'Has he left town?'

Marshal Stone nodded. 'Went in the same direction as Jake. He could be a heap of trouble to us unless he's stopped.'

He looked hard at the old miner. 'And as you keep tellin' me, Steve, you can hit anythin' you aims at.'

The eyes of the two men met in complete understanding.

Seven

Jake Cotter arrived home after an hour's ride. His house was an adobe building with several rooms and a wide veranda that was lined with comfortable wicker chairs. Old Abraham came out of the small bunkhouse to deal with the horses while Jake unloaded the wagon and carried everything into the coolness of a storeroom.

Abraham was a stooped man who had once been tall and straight. Years in the saddle had left him bow-legged, and as a widower with no family, his only home was at the Cotter farm. He was well looked-after, handled horses and cattle, but resolutely refused to have anything to do with pigs or milking. That was left to young Davy.

Davy was busy now, doing the evening chores while Jake and Abraham retired to the veranda to chew tobacco and talk of the day's events. There was a jug of corn whiskey and they shared it noisily as they looked out across the yard towards the setting sun.

'I was followed home,' Jake said casually.

'Was you now? And who would it be this time? Another fella who reckons you're goin' to lead him to a gold mine and make him rich?'

'I don't know who he is but he's a rat-faced character who was in the Golden Eagle and drinkin' with some of the locals.'

Abraham spat out a long stream of tobacco juice and hit a crawling bug, fair and square.

'Prospector, you reckon, or some hired gun?'

'Can't tell, but he'll sure as hell be watchin' us right now.'

Abraham grinned and displayed what were left of his blackened teeth.

'Maybe we should surprise him after dark,' he suggested. 'Sure would be a game to see if I could still sneak up on the coyote before he got a whiff of me.'

Jake laughed and spat some juice at another bug. He missed and pulled a face.

'I figure as how he'd get a whiff of you afore you moved a dozen yards,' he said cheerfully.

'Well, I know I ain't smellin pretty, but the steers don't mind, and the horses kinda enjoy it. Washing's for town folk, Jake, not for the likes of us. Do we bushwhack him?'

'I don't rightly know.' Jake Cotter scratched the side of his face. 'Depends what he's after and who he is.'

The mean-faced man was Walt McNally. He lay

behind a patch of mesquite and looked down the long slope at the house where two men sat chewing tobacco on the neat porch. Walt's leg was hurting him. It had never been right since that evening, over two years ago, when they had shot it out and only he survived. His right hand was partially crippled, though he could still use a gun, and the broken bone in his thigh had set badly. That was caused because of the delay before he could reach a doctor who would ask no questions.

It was six months before he was able to go back to the canyon with a wagon to move the loot from the army convoy. The shock of finding nothing there had been devastating. He had searched among the trees in a frenzy, and then sat by the stream for over an hour, trying to make sense of it. Nothing remained, and yet there had been no word said in the saloons and whorehouses about the military recovering their property. Somebody had stolen what belonged to him, and he was killing-mad about it.

He had searched throughout the territory, looking for someone who had suddenly become rich. He tried to pick up any little piece of information that might lead to the lost fortune that should have been his, and for which he had planned and killed so expertly. Elinor township had looked like a lead when three old-timers in a saloon had talked about Jake Cotter. The name meant nothing, but the man's sudden wealth needed investigation. Walt McNally lay in hiding and watched patiently.

The sun was rising above the distant hills when Jake Cotter harnessed the two mules, tied the store-bought goods to their panniers, and waved a hand in farewell to young Davy and old Abraham. He rode his large gelding and led the other two animals up the gentle slop of the valley towards the northern hills where the early mist still clung in a blue haze.

Walt McNally watched him go and then saddled his own horse to follow at a discreet distance.

The journey took up the best part of the day, to finally end at a fast-flowing stream that came down from a rocky slope and rattled over multi-coloured gravel towards a steep valley. Jake Cotter made camp for the night, cooked a meal, sat for a while in front of the fire, and then turned in amid the noises of the insects and animals that made their way to the running water.

He woke early, rinsed his face in the cold stream, and made himself a breakfast. Walt McNally watched everything, cursing that he could not light a fire or have a hot meal himself. He saw the shovel being unpacked along with a large copper dish, and realized that he was wasting his time. The man was panning for gold in the stream, and Walt had no ambitions to be a prospector. It meant hard work.

While Jake still laboured up to his knees in the cold water, the watcher quietly tightened the girth of his mount and led it out of earshot. His mean face was taut with anger at having wasted time on some silly old man who spent his days dredging up snippets of gold dust for a living. He mounted the horse and rode unhappily away.

One man saw him go. Old Steve Welling had tagged along behind the other two from the very start. He had watched Jake Cotter's house, seen the loading of the mules, and followed both men through the heat of the day to the quiet stream where Jake started panning.

Steve saw the mean-faced man riding off, and although tempted, decided not to bushwhack him in case the noise reached the ears of Jake Cotter.

He stayed on instead, lying on his belly and watching the prospector panning away under a hot sun. He decided by noon that it was time to report back to the marshal so that they could both share in the wealth of Jake Cotter's gold-bearing stream. He led his mules quietly away and headed back for Elinor.

He had gone about ten miles when a certain idea occurred to him. Jake Cotter was of no further use. The source of the gold had been located and only he and the marshal need know where it was. Old Steve halted in his tracks and thought about it. Jake Cotter had been a bad neighbour. He had found gold and kept the secret to himself. He had let down the whole town, and all his friends from the past.

The old man swung his mules round and began to head back for the stream. He reached down for the small bottle in the pocket of the folded trail-coat that lay across the saddle. It was cheap whiskey, but it tasted good. As he grew in courage, he even contemplated cutting out the marshal and keeping the secret all to himself. After all, he was getting on in years and this might be his last chance of a fortune.

It was early evening when he got back to the stream. He left the mules tethered to some bushes well out of earshot, and after checking his gun, moved very cautiously to the spot where he had lain earlier in the day. He was alert for every noise, but nothing disturbed the heavy air save the sounds of nature. As he peered carefully through a gap in a patch of stunted bushes, he could make out the silvery run of the stream as it flowed noisily over the valley floor. A few birds pecked at insects among the rocks while a buzzard hovered high above them.

Steve looked around for Jake Cotter. There was nobody about. Mules, horse, and prospector had all vanished, with only a few ashes from a burnt-out fire to indicate that they had ever been there.

Marshal Stone got up from his chair on the porch of the jailhouse. He could see the figure coming into town, riding one mule and leading another. It was old Steve Welling, dusty and tired, and with a bitterly disappointed look on his unshaven face.

He reined in opposite the lawman and got wearily down from his mount.

'Well?' The marshal's voice was taut.

'I followed 'em both,' the old man said fretfully. 'Followed 'em as true as true, and I saw the spot Jake Cotter was headed for. But he's done vanished, Marshal. Just got up and went.'

The lawman ushered him into the office and poured out hot coffee. While the old fellow was drinking it, Marshal Stone went outside and loosened the girths of the animals. He searched the pockets of the trailcoat and found the whiskey bottle. It was empty.

'So you lost him!' he snapped angrily when he re-entered the jailhouse.

'No, I never lost nobody. It weren't like that, Marshal.'

Steve explained what had happened but forgot to mention that he had gone back with the intention of killing Jake Cotter. The lawman listened impatiently, drubbing his fingers on the desk top as the tale was told.

'And do you reckon there's gold in that stream?' he asked when Steve stopped talking.

'Not a hope. I turned over the rocks and scooped up some gravel, but there ain't nothin' there that makes it look like gold-bearin' dust. I been prospectin' for forty years or more, Marshal, and that stream ain't no-how givin' out gold dust. I reckon that Jake was just leadin' us on.'

'So he knew he was bein' followed. That figures. He's nobody's fool. And this other fella – why did he leave when he saw him workin' the stream?'

Steve shook his head. 'I can't understand that. He seemed real upset because Jake was lookin' for gold. Sorta disappointed.'

The marshal heaved a sigh. 'You'd better take the mules round to the corral and go get yourself some sleep, Steve. I reckon we'll have to try again some time. Jake Cotter's one smart man. He led you to the wrong place and then moved on as soon as you left. He'll be back here in a few weeks with more dollars to put in the bank.'

'It sure riles me, Marshal,' the old prospector said as he stood up to go. 'He just ain't neighbourly.'

Brad Stone accompanied him to the door and stood there while man and mules vanished round the corner. Before he could return to the quietness of his office, he saw three figures bearing down on him. He muttered a curse before putting on a welcoming smile for the most important men in town. The lanky preacher led the way with his huge strides, the mayor on one side of him and banker Elijah Little on the other.

Otis Whiting had been mayor of Elinor township for three years – ever since he had bought drinks for the entire town at the election. The banker was one of his close friends, and both men had grown rich on their various deals in timber and quarrying.

They had other similarities too. Both were well dressed in big-city clothes, and with round, apparently honest faces that radiated confidence. The marshal sighed and ushered them into his office. The best whiskey had to be produced and the wooden chairs dusted over with a grubby piece of cloth.

'So, what's it all about?' the mayor asked without any preamble.

The marshal poured out the drinks before sitting down and telling what had happened. He experienced a feeling of virtue as he related the story. It made him appear the hero who was acting on behalf of the town. If gold had been found, old Steve Welling would probably have had enough sense to go round to the back door of the jailhouse, and the situation would have been quite different. The marshal would have said nothing.

The mayor shook his head in sorrow. 'It's a pity you failed, Marshal,' he said sadly. 'The community would have been in your debt if things had turned out better. We'll just have to go on waiting.'

The preacher murmured automatic agreement and added an 'Amen' for good measure.

'We need that gold,' the banker said emphatically. 'It would put this town back on the map.'

Eight

It was three weeks before Jake Cotter was seen again. He rode into Elinor on a tall bay gelding that bore a silver-mounted Mexican saddle. A hot wind was whipping down the main street as he dismounted in front of the bank and tethered the animal to the rail. His clothes under the dusty trailcoat were of unmistakable quality, and everything about him denoted a man of wealth.

He shook the dust off his hat and walked slowly up the wooden steps to enter the sacred portals of the only money-lending establishment in town. People stared at him coldly. Even old acquaintances frowned upon him as something of a traitor to the local community.

Jake just grinned and headed for the long, polished counter and the neatly dressed clerks. He took out a leather wallet from the deep pocket of his trailcoat and extracted a thick sheaf of banknotes. The man behind the counter took them eagerly, writing down the amount in a

73

ledger. He then entered details in the same neat hand on a page of the small red-backed book that Jake passed across.

While the transaction was being carried out, Elijah Little came out of his office. He pretended to be surprised at seeing Jake, and went across to shake hands.

'Haven't seen you in an age,' he said cheerfully. 'Come on in and have a drink.'

The clerk hurriedly lifted up a flap in the mahogany counter and Jake Cotter passed through to be guided into the neat office at the back of the building. It smelt strongly of cigars and beeswax polish, to which was quickly added the aroma of good-quality imported whiskey. The two men sat facing each other, glasses full and eyes watchfully alert.

'Y'know, Jake,' the manager said carefully, 'you and me have been friends for a good many years. And I value friendship. It's a great thing.'

Jake Cotter silently sipped his drink. His face was devoid of expression.

'And I reckon it's for friends to help each other.' The banker's face was beginning to drop sweat. 'You follow me?'

'I figure as how you're trying' to find out where I gets my money,' Jake said bluntly.

'No, no.' Elijah Little waved a dismissive hand. 'It wasn't like that at all. You see, Jake, money has to earn money, and folks like you and me, with a mite of capital, well – we have to invest. There's great opportunities for a man with a spare dollar or two. You could get yourself seriously rich if you had the right advice.'

'I ain't complainin' now,' Jake said unhelpfully.

'You got no need to. Not with all the money you have in this bank. But think about it, Jake. I could put you on to one or two deals in the quarrying business and the timber trade that would really make you rich. The territory is expanding, and it's people like us who can help the community. Invest in the right ventures and there's no limit to how wealthy you can become.'

'Sounds risky to me. I seen timber fellas go bust. And that quarry man over Mesa Verde way shot hisself when things went sour on him.'

'Ah, but they were badly advised, Jake. I make my investments with sound companies, and I'm in a position to put my friends on to some really good deals.'

He leaned across the desk with the whiskey bottle in his eager hand. Jake Cotter watched the glasses being refilled, but his face did not change expression.

'I'll think about it,' he said.

'Do that, Jake,' the banker urged. 'I'm not pressing you, but a man has to provide for the future, and you've a lot of money lying idle. Besides, you have a son. What about him?'

Jake's eyes brightened for a moment. 'What about him?' he managed to ask in a flat voice.

'Wouldn't it be something to leave him a real

big fortune? Better than punchin' cattle up Tombstone way. He could have a good life if you made the right moves.'

There was a long pause while both men toyed with their drinks.

'You got a point there, Elijah,' Jake Cotter eventually conceded, 'but I reckon as how young Tom will be the better for makin' his own way. It don't do for a man to get somethin' for nothin'. Don't seem natural. You gotta work for things.'

'Oh, sure, sure. But remember, Jake, your money comes from some source only known to you. Will Tom be able to tap that source when you pass on?'

Jake Cotter frowned and looked hard at the banker. He swallowed the last of his whiskey and rose to leave.

'You've given me somethin' to think about, Elijah,' he admitted, 'and I ain't sayin' as how you're wrong. Just let me think it over.'

'Sounds fair. Come and see me any time.'

'I'll do that. And one more thing. . . .'

'Yes, Jake?'

'You go gabbin' any more about my business, and I'll blow your fool head off.'

Jake Cotter rode home slowly, leaving a rather shaken banker pouring himself another glass of whiskey with an unsteady hand. Jake could not know that the mayor, the preacher, and several other members of the town council were discussing his affairs before he had gone a mile.

*

It was three weeks later that old Abraham set out to visit Elinor township to pay a call on the doctor for something to remedy the aches and pains of old age. Nothing ever seemed to help, but he had faith in the healing profession and he and the medical man believed in the same prescription for ageing bodies. They would both sit in the surgery, drinking old-fashioned corn mash and gossiping of days gone by. Abraham always felt better after this treatment, even though it seemed to make walking more difficult.

Davy and Jake stayed at home. The young man looked after the animals while Jake fished the creek or went out shooting for the pot. He had prepared a letter for his son, explaining a few things, and had left it in town to be picked up by the stage.

It was peaceful in the early evening as Jake Cotter sat on the porch chewing a wad of tobacco and watching the sun setting behind the smoky hills. He sighed contentedly and decided it was time to make a meal. Davy would soon be finishing the chores and the lamps would have to be lit.

He rose from the cane seat, stretched himself, and looked round the dusky scene with a feeling of pleasurable tiredness.

It was then that something caught his eye. It was a little flash of metal among the tall bushes across the valley. Something had reflected light from the last rays of the sun. He screwed up his eyes towards the slight haze of dust that was coming nearer as he watched. There were horsemen, three of them, and they rode tall animals that did not look quite like local cow ponies.

'Davy!' he called sharply. 'Stop that milkin' and come along here, young fella!'

The door of a long shed opened and a young man emerged, his fair hair long and unkempt as he ran across the yard to see what the boss wanted so urgently.

'What's up, Mr Cotter?' he asked eagerly.

The older man pointed to the cloud of dust and the vague outlines of the riders in the distance.

'Tell me what you see, boy,' he ordered. 'My eyes ain't what they used to be.'

The young man looked, one hand raised to shade his eyes from the fading sunlight.

'I figure as how they're Mexicans, boss,' he said quietly. 'Big horses and fancy saddles like what you've got. You expectin' 'em to come visiting?'

'Not so's you'd notice. Go inside, load a couple of scatter guns, and bring out my Colt.'

The young man did as he was told, part frightened, part excited at the prospect of trouble. He come out with the shotguns, handed one to Jake and stood with the other one cocked and ready in his own hands. He laid his boss's gunbelt on the wicker chair, and wore a gunbelt of his own with an old Colt .45 in the worn holster. His pants pockets were full of shotgun cartridges.

They waited for the riders to draw near, silently

listening to the steady beat of the hoofs that filled the air with reddish dust.

Something suddenly changed. One of the horsemen veered off to the left, another to the right, and only the centre one continued to head straight for the farm buildings. They were in clear sight now, and there was no doubt that trouble was their business.

Jake cocked the shotgun noisily and cursed under his breath.

'Get the hell off my land!' he shouted as soon as they were within earshot. He raised the gun and fired at the oncoming man who was now galloping his horse and was within sixty or seventy yards.

Davy was firing too, at the rider who had ridden over to the left. The horseman was coming round the cowshed, his large black mount flinging streams of sweat from its mouth as he used the reins to swing it hard over. The shot missed the rider and the cowshed door splintered as the charge threw out slivers of sun-bleached wood.

The youngster pulled the other trigger without really taking aim. The buckshot took the horse clear in the head and the animal reared agonizingly, throwing the rider to the ground.

Jake Cotter had also emptied the second barrel of his shotgun, but not at the oncoming horseman. He had been forced to swing round to counter the other rider who had gone off to the right. The charge of shot took the man in the shoulder but he managed to hold onto the reins. He was aiming a revolver and fired a single shot in return. It hit Jake in the chest and he staggered backwards before slumping to his knees. He tried to reach his own Colt where it lay on the chair, but another shot took him in the back and he collapsed on the veranda.

Davy had drawn his own pistol and fired three shots at the two men still on their horses. All of them missed and he went down in a hail of lead as the riders came within a few feet, emptying their guns into him before reloading to finish off Jake.

They got down from their mounts and looked around for any more opposition. The man who had come down from his injured horse was limping a little, and the one who had been hit in the shoulder by the spread of shot was nursing his arm and cursing in Spanish. All three stood on the veranda in the gathering dusk as though wondering what to do next.

Another rider suddenly appeared from behind one of the sheds. He was also on a large horse, but with a plain saddle that matched the neat drabness of the clothes he wore. He approached quite slowly while the men waited respectfully for him to alight.

'Only two of them?' he asked sharply in Spanish as he stood on the blood-soaked porch.

One of the men nodded and held out his hand eagerly. The newcomer reached inside his jacket and removed a flat package. He handed it over and the three men gather round while dollar bills were divided amongst them. One of the men pointed to his injured horse and seemed to demand extra compensation.

'There are plenty of horses here,' he was told brusquely. 'Help yourselves and get back across the border while you're still sober.'

He waited while the two who were still mounted went off to a nearby pasture to bring in a few cow ponies. The man on foot shot his injured animal and removed the saddlery.

When the three finally left, their employer stood silently for a few minutes as though savouring the cool darkness of the evening. Then he entered the farmhouse to light the lamps so that he could make a search.

Nine

Elijah Little sat complacently reading the ledger in front of him. It was like a work of literature to a man of his temperament. His large, handsome frame was bent over the desk, a cigar clamped in his teeth and a whiskey at his elbow. Business was good, and having the only bank in town, he dominated all the commerce of Elinor.

He looked up in annoyance when the clerk put his head round the door to announce a visitor. Then the banker's face cleared when he heard the name.

Tom Cotter had come home.

He rose from the chair to greet the young man who stepped through the door. Tom Cotter was in his late twenties, well built and tall, with dark hair, grey eyes, and a tanned face that was now covered in a slight coating of trail dust. His mouth was a straight, unsmiling line, set in a strong jaw that boded trouble for anybody who crossed him. His clothes were plain and he wore a serviceable Colt at his hip.

The two men shook hands as Tom took a seat in front of the desk and accepted the whiskey that was poured out for him. It was good whiskey because the Cotter family had a lot of money lodged in Elijah Little's bank.

'I'm sorry about your pa, Tom,' the banker said with what he hoped sounded like sincerity. 'He is surely a loss to the community. You got my letter then?'

'Yes, it caught up with me when we got back from the railhead. You didn't say much, other than that the farm had been raided and him and young Davy was shot. What happened to old Abraham?'

The manager shook his head sadly. 'He's safe enough but broken up by it, lad,' he said. 'Abraham had been in town to see Doc Carter, and when he got home again, he found them both dead and some of the horses missing. He came into town to tell the marshal, but we haven't seen him since. He might be at the farm. There are still cattle there to be looked after. If it's any consolation, your pa and the boy put up a fight. Somebody got himself wounded and there was a dead horse in the yard.'

'I'll go out there after I've rested up and settled his affairs. You said that he left quite a bit of money. Do I have to see a lawyer about things?'

'No, no. Your pa wasn't one for making wills. All his cash goes to you. When he started banking here about three years ago, he said that you were his only kin. So it's easy to handle. My only regret is that your father didn't have time to take my advice and invest in some of the local businesses. He was thinking about it when he was killed.'

He spread his hands in a gesture of despair.

'That's how things go,' he sighed. 'But you're looking well, Tom, and you've put on a bit of weight. The cattle business seems to suit you. But no more of working for other people now. You're a rich man, like your pa, and you can do whatever takes your fancy.'

He leaned forward confidentially and lowered his voice.

'Did your pa tell you about the mine?' he asked.

'What mine?'

The banker's face fell. 'Where his money comes from,' he said. 'He must have told you, lad. It's all a part of your inheritance.'

Tom Cotter thought about it for a moment. 'He sent me a letter a few weeks ago,' he said, 'but I only got it at the same time as I got yours. It just said that he believed that the folks in this town were not his friends any more and that he felt in danger. He told me that you were holdin' all his money, and that I was to keep Davy and Abraham on, whatever happened. And Abraham had to have a home for life.'

'Just like your pa,' Elijah Little intoned piously. 'Always thinking of other people.'

'Was it true?'

'Was what true?' the banker asked.

'About the folk round here givin' him reason to think he was in danger.'

'Ah, well, you see, Tom, your pa came into all this money, and folks were pretty sure he'd discovered gold. You know what that sort of thing does to people. They reckoned that as one of their own kind, brought up around here and knowing everybody all his life, your pa should have shared his find. Given everybody a chance after he'd registered his own claim. When they saw him coming into town a couple of times a year and banking large sums of money, they were mighty riled.'

'So they killed him?'

The banker recoiled as though struck a blow.

'Oh, no, Tom. Nothing like that. The men who raided the farm must have been strangers after a few horses. The only attempt to shoot him here in town wasn't even serious. Just an old drunk letting off steam. Old Steve Welling. You remember him?'

'Yes, he was one of pa's friends.'

'That's why it wasn't serious. He never meant to injure him. He was just making your father understand the feelings of the folks in town.'

The banker leaned forward with the whiskey bottle again but Tom Cotter put a hand over his still half-full glass.

'Well, I'll be gettin' out to the farm,' he said as he stood up.

Elijah Little got out of his own chair and escorted him to the door.

'I take it you'll be operating the mine and bringing in the cash just as your pa did,' he suggested tautly. 'We're always at your service, and it don't do to keep cash around the house.'

Tom Cotter looked at him coldly. 'I don't know where the mine is, Mr Little,' he said quietly. 'Pa sent me a letter but he didn't mention a mine. There might not be any more cash comin' in. He might have taken his secret with him.'

Tom had a meal at the Golden Eagle saloon while his two horses rested and fed at the livery stable. A few people spoke to him, remembering him from the past, but most chose to ignore Jake Cotter's son. Some even gave him a guilty look as they stood at the bar with glasses of cloudy beer in front of them. The town was upset by Jake's death. Some folk felt that their own attitude to the old man might have brought it about.

The preacher was the only one to make a really friendly approach. He waited until Tom emerged from the saloon to meet him on the wooden sidewalk and offer his condolence. He had known the young man from childhood and expressed his sorrow at all that had happened.

Tom shook him off as soon as he decently could and went round to collect his horses. He set off for home in an uncertain mood. He had got used to the idea of his father being dead, but the old man's letter had him puzzled. It had told him of the money in the bank, and of his duty to old

Abraham. It had also given him the name of a man he must visit in Tombstone. But that was all. Jake had been too cautious to tell anything that might be of value to any outsider.

He rode through the heat of the afternoon, down the long valley and into the fertile plain crossed by the streams that fed his father's land. There were a few cattle dotted about, and as he breasted a small rise, the farm buildings came into view. It was a pleasant aspect of a well-built farmhouse and outbuildings that looked welcoming after a long journey. The sun was nearly down by the time he reached the yard, with the shadows long and a slight wind sighing across the dusty earth.

He dismounted, loosened the girths on the horses, and crossed to the door of the house. It opened easily, letting out a current of warm, stale air. He entered wearily, carried his saddlebags to the table in the centre of the room and dropped them heavily on the slightly dusty surface.

Somebody chose that moment to put the barrel of a gun into the small of his back.

Ten

'You make a wrong move, fella, and you're one dead thief,' somebody said menacingly.

Tom Cotter heaved a sigh of relief. 'Abraham, you old goat!' he cried. 'I'd know that voice anywhere. And the smell. Now put your gun away before it goes off.'

The pressure of the barrel lessened and Tom turned slowly to confront the whiskered and sunburnt face of the old man. They both grinned a greeting as Abraham tucked the Colt .44 back in his belt. He embraced the young man warmly and then began lighting a double-wicked oil lamp that hung from the ceiling.

'Well, I sure didn't expect you just yet,' he said as he worked. 'Word was that you was up by the railhead, shippin' cattle to the north. You quit your job?'

'Sure did. It weren't the homecomin' I was hopin' for, but I reckon that my place is here from now on. Mr Little wrote me about pa's death, and

I rode into Elinor before comin' here. You were lucky not to be around at the time, Abraham.'

The old man was starting a fire in the stove and he turned angrily.

'Lucky be damned!' he snapped. 'Your pa and me was friends for nigh on forty years. It weren't no luck to be out of the fightin' that took his life. I weren't there the one time he needed me. What sort of blamed luck is that?'

'I know what you mean. Any idea who killed him?'

The fire was beginning to blaze and Abraham placed the coffee pot carefully in position. He stood back to admire his work before answering.

'And if I did know,' he said slowly, 'what would you do about it?'

The eyes of the two men met challengingly.

'I'd hunt 'em down and kill them,' Tom said firmly.

Old Abraham's grin returned. 'I hoped you'd say that, son,' he said happily. 'You take after your pa, and that ain't a bad thing. I can help you there. It's my fight too.'

'Abraham, you're too old. . . !'

The other man chuckled as he checked the coffee pot to see how it was getting on.

'Sure, I'm too old to go gallivantin' about lookin' for killers, but I ain't too old to put you on their tails.'

'You mean, you know who they are?'

'Not exactly, but I got a pointer that might help.'

'Did you tell the county sheriff and the town marshal?'

'Hell, no. What would they have done? It's just another killin' to them, and your pa weren't popular anyhows. I figured that you'd be turnin' up sooner or later, and you'd be eager to get some real justice done. Justice and law is two different things, boy, so we'll leave law to the lawyers while you and me gets some real honest justice handed out.'

Tom got some large cups down from a shelf and set them on the table.

'I reckon that's the way to go about it,' he agreed. 'Tell me what you know.'

'Well, I was in town that day, seein' Doc Carter about my roomytoid trouble. Him and me took a few drinks and I sorta floated back here some time after dark. Jake and Davy was dead on the porch out there, and this place had been torn apart like some fella was lookin' for somethin'. Real mess it were, and there was a dead horse just by the cow shed. Some of our ponies was missin', so I reckoned to them bein' horse-thieves.'

He made the coffee and the strong aroma filled the room. Both men stood silently for a few moments, their hands warming on the hot cups.

'And you've got some idea about who they are?' Tom asked quietly.

'Not exactly, but they left a dead horse behind and it had a brand,.'

'What brand?' Tom's voice was sharp.

'Don Diego Perez from across the border. You know the name, son?'

Tom nodded. 'If the old man is still alive, he's the straightest fella you could wish to meet. But he don't care for us *gringos*. Pa used to tell me that Don Diego always reckoned that all this territory belonged to Mexico.'

'That's the fella, and I reckon as how them horse-thieves stole some animals from him as well. He might know somethin' about them.'

'As I recall the tales told by my pa, he'd have been likely to kill them himself if he knew who they was.'

Abraham grinned. 'Not if they came this side of the border, son. This Diego fella don't cross into these United States. He's promised hisself not to do that until the land's restored to Mexico.'

Tom managed a grin as well. 'Then he'll wait one hell of a long time,' he said.

'I reckon so.'

'If that brand is the only lead we've got, I figure I'll just have to go south and talk with Don Diego. Will you be able to manage here?'

Abraham snorted. 'I'll survive,' he said gruffly. 'Always did and always will. But I need some help round the place. I bin a cattle man all my life and I don't take to milkin' cows and tendin' hogs and chickens. If folks knew I was doing things like that, I'd never be able to look 'em in the eye again. Tom Ransom's got a young son who'd be glad of a job. We could take him on at less than Davy was paid, and he'd be real happy to get away from that brute of a father.'

Tom nodded. 'You fix it up then, Abraham. You're in charge around here.'

The old man's eyes brightened a little. 'You're keepin' me on then?' he asked.

'For the rest of your life. Unless you aim to run out on me.'

'I ain't runnin' out, boy.'

'Then this is your home, just as pa intended, and I can ride down to Mexico. Tell me, Abraham, what do you know about this mine that folks is talkin' of?'

The old man screwed up his eyes. 'Ain't no mine,' he said huffily. 'Folks round here has one-track minds. A fella comes into a little money and they jump right into the bran tub. Your pa weren't no miner. He got his money somewheres else.'

'Do you know where?'

'Hell, no. The old coot was a great one for keepin' his own counsel. He never told me and I never asked. Didn't he say somethin' in that letter that was writ to you?'

'No. Just gave me the name of a fella in Tombstone. Ever heard tell of Jethro Flint?'

Old Abraham stared into the coffee cup as he concentrated.

'Yeah, I reckon I've heard that name. Your pa rode with him for quite a few years. Don't know whether he's still alive, though. Is he some sorta business partner with your old man?'

'Must be. I'm to visit him in Tombstone.'

Abraham shook his head in puzzlement. 'Looks like you got yourself some almighty travellin' to do, lad,' he chuckled.

Tom Cotter set out a couple of days later. He took two horses with him as well as a mule to carry the supplies. It was a forty mile journey due south and he had seldom been on the other side of the border. He was not quite sure of the location of the Diego Perez range, but it did cover a vast area and the local people would be able to help him on his way.

He moved at a steady pace, stopping frequently to cool the animals and rest in the heat of the day. The sky remained cloudlessly hard with the ground shimmering in the pitiless sun.

He was glad when, on the third day, a farmer told him that the next valley was the start of Don Diego's property. Tom halted on the crest of a hill and looked down on the sparse grass of the long, gentle slope that stretched for a couple of miles ahead of him. There were cattle over to the right, black and well-horned as they grazed near a small stream where the grass was in better condition.

After another two hours of riding, he came upon a slight rise in the ground, and there, on a fine plateau, was the estate of the Mexican landowner.

The buildings were all dazzlingly white, with

bright red roofs. They clustered round a vast courtyard guarded by a high wall and a wide gateway. Over to the left was a round structure, and Tom realized that he was looking at the first bullring that he had ever seen. There were pens around it and a nearby corral where some black cows chewed the cud as they watched him approach.

A man came from the house, halting for a moment on the wide veranda before walking down the steps to greet the visitor. He was a short man, but broad, with a dark, handsome face and greying moustache. His dress was very Mexican: well-cut short jacket, a white shirt held at the collar with two gold studs, and tight pants that ended in soft boots of good-quality leather.

'My house is your house,' he greeted Tom Cotter as he gestured him to dismount. The young man did so and explained who he was and the purpose of his visit. The older man's attitude underwent a subtle change. Where he had been coldly formal, he now smiled slightly and ushered the young man into the house. Two men came from a nearby building to look after the animals as Don Diego took his guest into the well-lit and sweet-smelling room that lay to the right of the main entrance of the hacienda.

A servant brought coffee and honey cakes while the conversation was at first of a general nature. Commiserations were offered over Jake's death as they drank the fragrant brew.

'I remember your father well,' Don Diego said in his good but rather sing-song English. 'He recovered cattle for us once or twice, when he was riding for Mr Wilson. Some of them followed the river line many miles further than usual in the drought years. Your father was a good man. He did not deserve to be taken by rustlers like the Pateca brothers.'

'You know them then, Don Diego?' Tom's eyes lit up as he nearly spilt the coffee.

'I know them. There were originally four but we caught one and hanged him. The others escaped into your—' he hesitated for a moment '—a part of the country. I was not able to follow them. If you do catch up with them I would be very gratified. I trust that is your intention?'

'It is. Have you any idea. . . ?'

'There is a little town just across the border – San Estaban. One of my people has seen the three brothers there on several occasions. The marshal is their cousin, so it makes a good centre for their activities.'

Tom nodded slowly and then put a delicate question.

'Why haven't you sent your people in to get them, Don Diego?' he asked.

'If I cannot go myself, I do not employ assassins to do the work for me. I must wait until they come back here, or until somebody like you arrives who also has a crime to avenge.'

'I get your point. I'll certain sure be gunnin' for

them, and thanks for your help.'

'You are welcome. They took twelve of my best saddle horses. Bigger and better animals than any you have in your – on your side of the border. I breed bulls and horses as well as farming beef cattle. The bulls and the horses are precious to me.'

'Yeah, those animals I saw on my way here. Down by the river. They don't look like no cattle I've ever seen before.'

Don Diego's dark eyes lit up. 'They are fighting bulls,' he said proudly. 'My family has bred them from Spanish stock for more than sixty years. I supply the local bullrings, but now that the railroad is getting closer, I am hoping that their fame will spread to other parts of the country.'

'That bullring, at the side of the house, is that where they fight?'

'No, no. That is a *tienta* ring. It is where we test the cows for bravery. A bull gets its courage from its mother and its beautiful conformation from its sire. The bulls are never fought until they enter the ring.'

'They don't seem to have much of a life, do they?'

The older man laughed, displaying small white teeth beneath the heavy moustache.

'They have a fine life,' he said. 'Much longer than the beef cattle, and when they die, they go out in a blaze of glory. They fight because it is their nature, and they believe that they will always conquer. No miserable slaughterhouse for them. I would be very content to die like one of my brave bulls. Your world is very different, *gr* – young man.'

He stood up and a servant appeared as if by magic.

'Now, you must stay the night and rest. You have a long journey ahead of you. Do you know where San Estaban is?'

Tom nodded. 'I've never been there, but it's just east of Nogales, on Almaretto Creek,' he said. 'I'll find it.'

'Then take care. The Pateca brothers are dangerous.'

Tom Cotter smiled slightly. 'So am I,' he said.

Eleven

Tom Cotter left the Perez spread early the next morning. They had lodged him comfortably in a bunkhouse that looked out over the fields. The food was oily but he had tasted worse from cooks on the range, and the beans were much the same north or south of the border. Don Diego saw him off, waving politely as the young American turned under the arch and led his animals back along the trail to the frontier.

San Estaban was a tiny townlet, built along the edge of a narrow creek that flowed from a low range of hills to the east. The houses were all in the Mexican style: whitened adobe with tiled roofs, and lining no more than three or four rutted streets. There was one cantina, that served as a hotel, a large church with a graveyard attached, and a few small stores that sold the bare necessities.

The marshal's office was little different than the rest of the buildings. It was a small place that needed a new coat of whitening and had windows that carried heavy but rusty bars.

It took Tom Cotter two days to reach San Estaban, and the journey had given him time to work out a strategy. He stopped at the edge of town, spotted the livery stable and took his mounts there to be cared for while he found what he was seeking. He checked the Colt at his belt, tucked the Winchester under one arm, and set off down the street for the jailhouse. It was nearly noon, the sun was hot, and even a couple of scruffy-looking dogs were lying in the shade as if exhausted.

The door of the jailhouse was open to let in some air, and behind a pale, worn desk, the marshal sat with his arms folded and his feet stretched out as he snored gently. His gun lay in its holster on the desk top and Tom Cotter grinned as he looked round the little room. It was shabby, with a single oil lamp hanging from the ceiling. The gun rack bore only two old Spencer rifles, a shotgun, and a few boxes of ammunition. There were some notices pinned to a board and an unlit stove with a white enamel coffee pot on top of it. There was a cell in the far wall, unoccupied and housing a bare wooden cot with a chair next to it. The place smelled of decay and old cooking oil.

Tom took a badge from the pocket of his shirt and pinned it carefully on his leather waistcoat. He stood in front of the desk and rapped sharply on the woodwork with his knuckles.

The marshal awoke with alarm. He was a short man, very dark, with several days' growth of beard, and black hair that came low across his forehead. His belly wobbled as he straightened up in the chair to stare with startled eyes at the noisy intruder.

'I'm lookin' for the Pateca brothers,' Tom Cotter said without preamble. 'They use your town as their hideout.'

The marshal stared at him as if not understanding what was being said.

'Pateca brothers,' he repeated. 'I – I don't know them.'

'You're their cousin.'

The man blinked. 'Oh, them. The name didn't come to mind for a moment. We're not really related. Just distant kin.'

'Kissin' cousins?'

'Kissin'? Oh, you're makin' a joke. Very funny.' The man stood up and there was sweat on his brow. 'Why do you want them?'

'Stealing horses. Killing people. The usual things.'

The marshal leaned forward across the desk to peer at the badge. He swallowed noisily.

'You're a County Sheriff?'

'That's what it says, and me and my posse are lookin' for the Pateca brothers.'

'They ain't here.'

'Is that a fact?'

The marshal shook his head and his belly wobbled almost in time to the movement.

'Left long ago,' he said earnestly. 'I ran them outa town.'

Tom Cotter smiled. 'You must be one tough fella,' he said admiringly. 'Got the keys to that cell?'

'Sure. Why?'

'I aim to put you behind bars. If the Pateca brothers are not in town, I'll maybe let you out again. If they are – you're like to be behind bars for quite a few years. Now, move.'

The marshal hurriedly opened the top drawer of the desk, and under Tom's watchful eye, he took out the key, unfastened the cell, and quietly placed himself inside. The young man locked the door and slipped the key in the pocket of his pants.

'Now, just stay quiet, or I'll have one of my men beat you around the head with a gun butt,' he said warningly.

The marshal nodded dumbly and sat down on the cot.

Tom Cotter left the jailhouse and stood for a moment in the middle of the main street. There was a saloon down on the left-hand side with a few horses tethered on the hitching rail. He walked slowly down and examined each one. None of them bore the brands he was looking for and only one carried a Mexican saddle. The others all bore old army equipment, including a couple of ancient McClellan saddles.

He went into the cantina and looked around. There were no more than a dozen customers, but none of them appeared remotely like desperate criminals of Mexican origin. He received a few hostile glances but the sight of the badge silenced any remarks that might have been on the lips of the drinkers. Tom left the men in peace and walked round the back of the buildings where several corrals were situated. He looked at the horses there but all of them were scruffy cow ponies.

At a loss about what to do next, he wandered among the houses and back to the main street. It was still quiet as he crossed between two stores to look for any other horses that might bear the brands he was seeking. He was beginning to sweat, partly with the heat, but also because he feared the marshal might summon up the courage to start shouting for help. It was then that he spotted a small mission hut and the black-clad preacher pinning up a notice on the wooden door.

'Excuse me, Reverend,' he said politely, 'but I'm lookin' for some fellas by the name of Pateca, or some horses that might have a JC or DP brand on them.'

The preacher was a short, stout man with a pale face topped by gold-rimmed glasses. He blinked at the young visitor through moist eyes and noticed the badge he wore.

'If you'd care to come inside,' he said quietly as

he looked carefully around, 'I might be able to assist you.'

He pushed open the door and stepped aside so that Tom could enter the little hut with its rows of worn chairs. Light came brightly through clean windows and the place smelt of bleach and soap. The door closed behind them and the preacher put a chubby finger to his lips.

'You don't mention the name of Pateca round here,' he warned. 'They are very dangerous men, and the marshal is kin to them. Now, how can I help you without getting my head shot off?'

'Just tell me where they're likely to be.'

'Have you a posse?'

'No, I'm by myself.'

The preacher shook his head in despair. 'You're a very brave young man,' he said, 'or a very foolish one.'

Tom grinned. 'I'm certainly foolish,' he agreed, 'but I got me a personal thing against the Patecas. They killed my pa, and stole some of our horses.'

The preacher took out a large silver watch and flipped the case open.

'They'll be having a meal at this time of day,' he said. 'They lodge at Ma Furbin's boarding house at the north end of town. It's just behind the main street and there's a corral built on to the side of it. Her husband used to deal in mules.'

Tom nodded his thanks. 'And their horses?' he asked.

The preacher managed a smile. 'Two of them

are riding fine animals with a DP brand on them, but the P has been changed to a B. The youngest brother has a cow pony now. It's a bay gelding with a JC brand. Watch out for them, Sheriff. They're evil men.'

'I'm very grateful for your help, Reverend. Do you happen to know what was done with the other horses they stole from Don Diego Perez and my pa?'

The preacher pursed his lips. 'I guess they sold them around town,' he said grimly. 'Everybody would know they were stolen, but the Patecas run this place like it was their own kingdom. When they offer a horse for sale, it takes a brave man to turn them down.'

'Have any of them been injured recently?'

'Yes, the youngest one. Chico, they call him. He came back here with a gunshot wound in the shoulder a few weeks back. Antonio was riding that gelding. When they left, he was on one of the fine big horses like his accursed brothers.'

'Well, thanks, Reverend. Just one more thing. How many boarders does Ma Furbin have?'

'Just the Patecas. Nobody else would stay in the same house as them. They've forced themselves on her.'

Tom nodded his thanks once again and left the cool building. The street was still quiet and there was no sigh of life at the jailhouse. He headed for the north end of the little town and easily found the boarding house. It bore a sign advertising vacancies and was a neat place with clean lace curtains on shining windows. There were only two horses in the nearby corral. One was a large black mare with a DB brand, while the other was a bay gelding cow pony clearly bearing Jake Cotter's mark. Tom checked his guns before going quietly round to the back door of the building.

He listened at the kitchen and could hear a woman gently singing to herself as she washed dishes that rattled in an enamel bowl. He glanced in the window to catch a glimpse of a stout, pale-faced woman whose grey hair was tied back in a bun. He tapped softly on the back door and waited patiently until she opened it, wiping her hands on an apron as she stood in the entrance.

He pointed at the badge he was wearing as he put a finger to his lips.

'How many of the Pateca brothers are in there, ma'am?' he asked quietly.

'You come to take 'em in?' she asked in return with a slight note of hope in her voice.

'Yes, ma'am.'

'Well, thank God somebody's doin' somethin' about them! Antonio's just finishin' his meal and Chico has gone up to their room. He's got a hurt arm and ain't feelin' too good. The devil rot him!'

'And the third one?'

'Manuel went out about half an hour ago. Gone visitin' his woman in Palos Verde.'

Tom nodded. 'Well, ma'am,' he suggested, 'if you was to take a walk around town for a few minutes,

I reckon you'd be free of your boarders by the time you got back home.'

She chuckled, her pale face a little flushed. 'And miss seein' 'em get what's comin'? No siree! I aim to see you kill 'em. You are goin' to kill 'em, I hope? All them trials and lawyers is just a waste of public money.'

'I'll be killlin' them, ma'am. You just stay here then.'

She pointed out the room across a narrow hall where Antonio Pateca was still eating his meal.

The young Mexican got a shock when the door suddenly opened and he found himself facing an armed man. His own gun was at his side but he was seated and his right hand held a cup of coffee. Antonio Pateca was a short, slim man with dark features and a neat moustache above a mouth that bore prominent white teeth. He half rose from his chair and then sat down again as he stared at the Winchester that Tom Cotter held in the crook of his arm.

'And who the hell are you?' the Mexican asked in good English. 'We got ourselves a lawman in this town.'

'He's been dealt with,' Tom said unhelpfully. 'Now it's your turn. You and your two brothers killed my pa and a young fella what worked for him. Then you stole some of our horses. I've come for you.'

'Your pa? And who the hell would he be?'

'Jake Cotter of the JC spread. Up north by

Elinor township. You remember now?'

The man clearly did. He put down the coffee cup and his right hand moved towards the edge of the table.

'I don't know nothin' about it,' he said sullenly. 'You got yourself the wrong man, fella.'

'Have I? One of your brothers is ridin' a horse that was stole from us and you got one of Don Diego Perez's animals out in the corral.'

The Mexican rose slowly to his feet. The distance between the two men was no more than six or seven feet.

'You sure is one nose-pokin' fella,' he sneered, 'but I ain't easy to take, so you'd better know how to use that gun.'

Antonio Pateca had already noted that the Winchester was not cocked. He reached down for the Colt at his side and slid it into view, hammer back and finger on the trigger. There was a loud explosion and Tom Cotter staggered back against the door.

Twelve

The only sound in the room was a steady dripping noise. Tom Cotter got slowly to his feet, his left arm throbbing as blood trickled from his fingertips on to the thick carpet. He suddenly realized that Antonio Pateca was sitting down again. The man lay back in his chair, his eyes wide open and a blank expression on his dark face.

It was his blood that was dripping on to a part of the floor not covered by the carpet.

Tom looked at the Winchester where it lay at his feet. He had not fired a shot. He heard footsteps on the stairs and pulled himself together. The youngest Pateca brother was coming, and Tom drew his Colt .44 and stood against the wall as the door flew open.

The young Mexican was a slim man with long, unwashed hair that flared round his head as he burst into the room. He saw his opponent too late, and even as he pulled the trigger of the gun without taking proper aim, Tom Cotter shot him in the chest. The youth tumbled to his knees, tried to recover, and then sank down with a slight moan.

Ma Furbin called out from the kitchen. Her voice was anxious, but Tom was able to assure her that everything was all right. She came in with a bowl of hot water and checked the wound in his arm. The two dead men did not seem to affect her in the least as she cut linen for bandages and bathed the wound.

'You ain't hurt worth a damn, Sheriff,' she said cheerfully. 'Just a flesh wound. I seen far worse in my day. There ain't even a bullet to take out. It's gone and bedded itself in my new wallpaper. And you sure took care of them two.'

Tom stood quietly as she worked. He was looking at the window and had seen the hole that sprang up just level with Antonio Pateca's back. The man had been shot from somewhere out near the corral. A bullet went through his spine just as he had drawn on Tom.

While Ma Furbin worked, there was a commotion from the kitchen as several people forced their way in, each struggling to be first to see what was happening. Tom Cotter found to his surprise that he was a local hero. The mayor introduced himself while a medical man checked on Ma Furbin's work, pronounced it well done, and joined in the congratulations that were showered on the injured man.

'There's still one of them alive,' Ma Furbin warned the mayor. 'He's over at Palos Verde.'

'Ah, but only one, dear lady,' the First Citizen replied cheerfully. 'And now that our marshal is already locked up, we can leave him there and get ourselves a new lawman. There's hope for this town at last.'

He turned to Tom Cotter, who was now being pressed to take a glass of whiskey.

'Perhaps you'd care for the job, Sheriff?' he suggested.

The young man shook his head. 'No, thanks, Mr Mayor. It's good of you to offer, but I'm not a lawman.'

The mayor looked at the badge and raised his eyebrows.

'I picked that up a few years back,' Tom explained. 'I'm a cowpoke, tryin' to get even with the men who killed my pa. Two are dead, but I still aim to finish with this Manuel fella. Then I'm on my way. Those horses in the corral – one belongs to Don Diego Perez, and the other is mine. You mind if I take them?'

Nobody minded, and Tom Cotter was on his way half an hour later, with the best wishes of the community and two extra animals behind him.

He was puzzled. Somebody had saved his life back there, but nobody had come forward to claim the credit. He looked behind him several times in case he was being followed, but the trail seemed clear as he made his way to Palos Verde.

Palos Verde was an even smaller place than San

Estaban. It lay almost on the Mexican border and most of its inhabitants spoke Spanish. There were no real streets – just a jumble of adobe houses, a small cantina, and a church that bore a little tower that housed a large bronze bell. There seemed to be nobody about although the heat of the day had passed. Tom Cotter looked vainly for a livery stable of some sort, and eventually had to settle for leaving his animals tethered to a large tree that shaded the communal well.

He walked across to the cantina and entered. It was dim and cool with a strong smell of grease that mingled with the reek of cheap alcohol. The bar was a few wooden planks atop a couple of barrels, and the few tables seated half a dozen Mexicans who looked up without curiosity at the stranger who entered.

The barman was the only one interested in Tom Cotter. He smiled a welcome until he saw the sheriff's badge. Then his fat face closed up to an impassive stare.

'You want a drink?' he asked bleakly.

'Where's Manuel Pateca?' Tom Cotter's voice was hard as he held the Winchester pointing at the man's belly.

'I don't know a Manuel Pateca,' the barman said sullenly.

'Could you use fifty dollars reward money?' Tom asked.

The closed face suddenly relaxed and the man leaned forward across the bar to whisper.

'He's with Dolores in the room at the top of the stairs,' he said softly. 'Been there an hour.'

Tom nodded and walked up the narrow, creaking staircase to the upper floor. The door was so flimsy that one good kick with a boot would burst it wide open. He checked the Winchester and raised his foot.

The blow sent the door crashing against the wall as it flew open to disclose the small bedroom. There was a shrill scream and a curse from a deeper voice as Tom Cotter stood framed in the doorway pointing the gun at the naked occupants of the bed. His glance took in the gunbelt and holster on the floor with the man's clothes beside them.

'You're Manuel Pateca?' he asked calmly.

The man nodded dumbly. He was older than his brothers, with a hairy body and dark, narrow face that was clean-shaven but bore long sideburns of jet black hair. The eyes were hard, and as cold as those of his opponent.

'I'm Pateca,' he said in good English, 'and who the hell are you?'

'Jake Cotter's son.'

The man frowned. 'And who is Jake Cotter?' he asked.

'A man you killed up near Elinor. You and your brothers raided a ranch there; shot an old man and a boy just to steal a few ponies.'

Manuel Pateca looked puzzled for a moment and then his brow cleared.

'Oh, I recall it now. them two put up a fight. Chico got winged and we lost a good horse. Anyway, what's your interest?'

He could not see the sheriff's badge in the dimness of the room, but he could see the Winchester clearly enough and was edging towards the pile of clothes on the floor. Tom Cotter motioned with the rifle.

'If you make a move for your gun,' he said flatly, 'I'll kill you, sure as sure. So don't get any ideas. Does the girl speak English?'

'No.'

'Tell her to take her clothes and get the hell outa here.'

Pateca muttered a few words to the girl and she hurriedly leapt out of the bed, grabbed her dress and a pair of slippers from the floor and scampered out of the room.

'What do you aim to do?' the Mexican asked tautly.

'You killed my pa, so I'm killin' you.'

'My brothers will hunt you down, fella. We're a pretty revengeful family.'

'They're dead. I left them in San Estaban. And your cousin is locked in his own jailhouse.'

The narrow face darkened with anger. 'You sure have one hell of a nerve for a hick farm boy. You got me cold right now, but if I had a gun at my side. . . !'

'You'll have a chance, fella. Now, get outa that bed and go stand in the corner. Away from the window.'

The man looked as if he was going to argue the point for a moment. Then he complied and stood naked against the lime-washed wall. Tom Cotter picked up the holster, emptied the shells from the gun and dropped it on the bed.

'Now, all you gotta do is to get yourself dressed, load your gun, and meet me on the street,' he said grimly. 'I ain't an old man or a young lad.'

He turned to open the door and then remembered a question he needed to pose.

'Why did you search the house?' he asked. 'And why didn't you take the few dollars that were there?'

Pateca shook his head. 'I never searched the house,' he said. 'That must have been the fella what hired us. We just rounded up a few horses and lit out. Chico needed a doctor fast.'

Tom Cotter stared at the man in disbelief.

'You was paid to raid the JC ranch?' he asked in wonderment.

'Sure. You think we'd waste our time travellin' so far north just to steal a few animals?'

'Who paid you?'

The man shrugged. 'How the hell would I know? And why should I tell you, anyways?'

'Maybe you could live longer.'

Manuel Pateca thought it over for a moment.

'Look, fella,' he said in a friendlier voice, 'we was hired by some *gringo* to go north, raid this ranch, and make sure that the owner got hisself killed. I didn't ask questions and the fella paid up handsomely as soon as we'd done the job. He stayed behind to search the place, and that's all I can tell you.'

'No name?'

The man grinned. 'What do you think?'

'So what did he look like, and what sort of horse was he riding?'

Manuel Pateca shook his head. 'He played fair and I ain't sayin' more. Get the hell out if you ain't satisfied. I'll be down as soon as I'm dressed.'

Tom Cotter nodded and left the room. He went slowly down the stairs, past the glances of the customers in the cantina, and walked a dozen yards away to stand waiting impatiently for Manuel Pateca. He had a feeling that the man might duck out of a rear window, collect his horse and make a break for it. It did not seem to matter any more. He now had a more important riddle to solve. Who had hired the man to kill his father? And why?

Tom glanced up at the angle of the sun to make sure that it would not be in his eyes when the shooting started. He laid the Winchester on the ground and checked the Colt at his side. A few people were gathering in the distance as though they had heard what was going to happen. He wondered if there was a marshal, but the place seemed to be too small for any sort of authority. Figures began to emerge from the cantina. They lined up as though for a photograph against the white wall, with the bartender standing in the centre.

Then Manuel Pateca came through the doorway. He blinked for a moment in the bright sun before turning in the direction of his adversary and stepping out into what passed for the main street. He walked confidently, his right hand tensed and his eyes narrowed and alert.

Tom Cotter waited without moving. He watched the gun hand as the man came nearer. His own fingers were ready to grasp the butt of the Colt and pull back the hammer as soon as Pateca made a move.

A silence had fallen and not even a bird seemed brave enough to sing. It was at that moment that Tom heard a sound behind him. It was an indefinable noise. He felt a chill as he realized that Pateca might have arranged for somebody to bushwhack him. He shifted a little to the right, watching every move of the Mexican while trying to angle himself into a position where he could see the source of the noise.

He recognized it now. It was a horse, moving on the rutted dirt with a faint jingle of harness. He heaved a sigh of relief. It would be somebody coming into town – not a friend of Manuel Pateca skulking in ambush. He could concentrate on the man in front of him.

Pateca made a dive for his gun at that moment. Tom drew as well, and the Mexican staggered backwards before either of them got off a shot.

Thirteen

It was the horseman who fired. His animal stood motionless as he levelled the rifle and shot Manuel Pateca neatly through the chest. Before anyone on the street could move, he swung his mount round and galloped off in a cloud of dust. There was no way of identifying the figure. Just a dark man on a dark horse, silhouetted against the harsh sun.

Tom Cotter looked round for a saddled animal, but there was none in sight. His own horses were fifty yards away, their girths loosened and their bellies full of water. He had no chance of catching up with the killer, and stood there looking as stupid as the rest of the townsfolk.

The bartender went slowly across to the dead bandit and looked down at the body. Then he moved over to where Tom still stood with the unfired pistol in his hand. There was a slight smile on the man's round face.

'You said there was a reward, Sheriff,' he muttered. 'Fifty dollars.'

Tom Cotter pulled himself together. 'Take his body to the new marshal in San Estaban,' he advised. 'He'll pay up. If you tell him you killed Manuel Pateca, you'll be a hero.'

He walked back to his horses and began tightening their girths. Nobody seemed interested in him as he left town in the same direction that the killer had taken. There was no hope of catching up with the man, but he kept a sharp lookout in case he was being trailed or could be the victim of an ambush. He did not much care for the idea of a mysterious guardian angel.

He stopped off at his own ranch before going on to Tombstone. Abraham was running things as usual and a young lad was doing the milking and other odd jobs. Tom Cotter was glad of a good meal in front of his own stove. He told the story to Abraham while the old man listened carefully as he chewed tobacco and drank his corn mash.

'You sure is one lucky fella,' he said cheerfully. 'Whoever is trailin' you certainly don't want you dead. I suppose you know why?'

'The gold mine all the local folks think I own?'

'Sure as shootin'. If you die, the secret dies with you, son. And they can't have that. You had a visitor the other day. Mayor Whiting, and he was awful keen to see you. Wants you to call into town as soon as you can.'

'Any idea why?'

Old Abraham shrugged. 'Wouldn't tell the hired help, but he looked one worried man. It's gotta be important for him to ride out here.'

'I'll call into town on the way to Tombstone.'

The meeting took place in the mayoral office. Marshal Stone, Preacher Bride, the banker, and some of the other prominent citizens sat around the large desk. The air was filled with tobacco smoke and the fumes of good whiskey as they confronted Tom Cotter. Marshal Stone was left to do the talking.

'It's this way, lad,' he said urgently. 'Folks are starting to leave town. There ain't nothin' here no more for young people. Stores is closin', the timber business ain't what it was, and families are beginning to move west to Texas. They figure that there ain't no future in Elinor.'

'So what's this to do with me?' Tom asked sharply.

'Your pa could have helped his neighbours. They all reckon he let them down. Now, we gotta look to you to bring this town alive once more. We need that gold fever again. Just like the old days.'

Tom Cotter looked at the faces round the desk. There was a mixture of worry and greed on them. He trusted nobody in Elinor township.

'My pa was murdered by three men,' he said slowly as he watched their expressions. 'They're all dead, but that ain't enough. They was paid to do it. Some fella actually bought my pa's death. Now, who would that be?'

The marshal looked hard at the young man.

'They didn't know who hired them?' he asked.

'No. Just a fella with cash money. Tell me, Marshal, has anybody been away from town this last week or so?'

The lawman lowered his eyes as Tom stared hard at him. The others seemed equally anxious to look out of the window.

'I don't recall anybody bein' away for any time,' Marshal Stone said carefully. 'Why?'

'Somebody's been trailin' me. Somebody who seems to want to keep me alive. Strange, ain't it? My pa gets shot, but someone is tryin' desperate hard to make sure I don't get killed.'

The mayor broke the ensuing silence by pouring out more of his whiskey.

'What plans have you in mind, Tom?' he asked with attempted cheeriness.

'Oh, I got another trip to make and then I'll be settling down on our spread and giving old Abraham a hand round the place. I reckon to make it a real workin' ranch. The pasture seems to be pretty good out there.'

The conversation began to peter out and Tom Cotter left shortly afterwards. He bought a few supplies, called in at the bank to collect some money for expenses, and then went round to the livery stable to collect his horse and mule. The preacher was there, talking to the owner. He seemed to have been waiting for Tom, and as the young man saddled up, the Reverend Bride helped him.

'I'm worried, Tom,' the preacher said softly. 'This town is greedy and frightened. You heard them in there, and they're the more intelligent ones. Can you imagine what the rest of the folk are feeling?'

'Of course I can. They want my pa's gold, but I don't know where it is. It might not even exist.'

'And if it does?'

'Reverend,' Tom said feelingly, 'if there is a mine and I find out about it, you have my word that once I've staked my claim and one for Abraham, I'll tell the whole town where it's located.'

'You're a good lad, Tom. It would give us all a new hope. But guard yourself. Don't trust any of them.'

'I don't. They was actin' pretty shifty back there.'

The preacher hesitated. 'You asked if anybody had been missing from town since you were last here,' he said quietly. 'The marshal got back this morning. He's been looking into a bit of rustling over at Will Foster's place. The mayor and Elijah Little have also been away. Some business dealings, so I'm told. They came back last night. They're a pretty close bunch that run this town, and the last thing they want right now is for you to be killed.'

'I see that, Reverend, but who wanted my pa dead?'

The preacher shook his head sadly. 'I think I know why that occurred,' he said. 'Your father was a stubborn man. He wasn't going to help the town, whatever happened. But if he died and passed on the secret to you, they thought that maybe you'd be more willing to help.'

Tom took a deep breath. 'And you think one of our prominent citizens killed my pa so that I'd come back and lead 'em to the gold?'

'I may be wrong, but that's how I see it. It isn't Christian, but it's very human, my boy.'

'I'll have to think about this,' Tom said quietly. 'You and me will have another talk some time soon.'

Tombstone was a long journey. It took Tom Cotter three days before he passed round the edge of the salt flats and found himself in sight of town. He got a place to stay on the outskirts, stabling his mule and spare horse before riding along Allen Street to the junction with Fourth. He did not really know the town but directions in his father's letter were clear.

Brown's Hotel stood on the corner, and next to it was a gun shop. It was not the one he was looking for, but he had been told to ride north from that spot to another store on the left-hand side of the street.

It was easy to find, but to his surprise, was closed. The green blinds were down over the double doors and the windows bore wooden shutters. He looked up at the gold-leafed lettering that displayed the name of Jethro Flint. Somebody seemed to live above. The upper windows were clean and heavily curtained with yellow net. He hammered on the door and waited patiently.

Nothing happened, though as he stepped back on the boardwalk, there seemed to be a little twitch at one of the curtains. Tom gave another loud knock, and after a long pause, the green blind moved aside a little and the face of an elderly woman peered at him through the glass. Her features were pale, framed in grey hair, and there was a pinched expression round her eyes.

'Who are you?' she mouthed through the glass door panel.

'Tom Cotter. Jake's son,' the young man shouted back. 'My pa's dead and he wrote me to come here.'

The blind closed up again and there was silence for a while. Then another face appeared. It was that of a thin, elderly man, unshaven and frightened. He was bald save for a fringe of grey hair round the back and sides of his head. He scrutinized Tom silently for a moment before opening the door and pulling him hurriedly inside.

'Was you followed here, lad?' he asked urgently.

'I aim not to be,' Tom replied, 'but it ain't difficult to trail somebody if you've a mind to. You Jethro Flint?'

'I sure am, and I recognize you from that photograph thing your pa showed me. Remember it?'

Tom grinned. 'Me holdin' the prize at the turkey shoot five years back?'

The man holstered the gun he was carrying. 'That's the one, and if you know'd about that, I reckon you're Jake's boy. I was sure sorry to hear about your pa. We rode together for six years or more. Couldn't have had a better partner. You'll take coffee with us, son?'

They went through the darkened shop to comfortable rooms upstairs. Mrs Flint poured out strong coffee and the two men sat opposite each other in the well-lit room.

'Your old man told me that when he died, he'd leave orders for you to make contact,' Jethro said between sips. 'He didn't trust nobody else. Him and me was partners in this thing and we figure to keep it just between the two families. If anything happens to me, I gotta rely on you to look after Sal here. You understand that?'

'I sure do,' Tom nodded, 'but is this really a gold mine like folks in Elinor keep saying?'

Jethro shook his head violently. 'There ain't no gold, boy. Nary a single nugget. But it don't do no harm to let 'em think it's a mine we have. The real truth is more dangerous. 'Specially now I got a killer on my tail, and if he spots you, he'll sure as hell add your scalp to his belt.'

'You'd better tell me what I'm gettin' into, Mr Flint.'

'I reckon as how I'd better do just that thing. And call me Jethro. Sounds more homely.'

He wiped his mouth with a rough, hairy hand before pouring himself more coffee.

'It started nearly three years ago. Your pa and me was ridin' for Mr Wilson. We was out roundin' up strays to join a drive to the railhead, and we spotted this little canyon where a few cattle had wandered to get at the water. There was a line of trees along one wall, and behind them was a load of guns, saddles, ammunition, sabres, and that new dynamite stuff they use for quarryin'. At least twenty or thirty thousand dollars' worth. It was unbelievable. Your pa knew what it was right away. A military wagon train had been bushwhacked a few months earlier and all this stuff had been stolen. All the raiders were dead. They had a shoot-out among themselves up near Manston. Someone had read about it in a Tombstone newspaper and told your pa.

'Well, the army hadn't found it; the folk who put it there was dead; so we reckoned as how we'd discovered a good way of makin' sure we had ourselves a comfortable old age. We started sellin' off the stuff a bit at a time over the border. Not bein' greedy, but just takin' a little on each trip, and sellin' to them Mexican fellas who weren't goin' to ask questions if the price was right.'

He paused to cross nervously to the window and look out on the street below.

'We moved the stuff from the canyon, of course. Put it in a mine shaft along the Nepa Valley where nobody ever goes these days. We'd arrange to meet about twice a year, make like we was prospectin', and take a few things across the border. We sure had one fine set-up. Until now.'

'And now you're runnin' scared of something?'

'I sure am, lad. Them raiders didn't all die in the shoot-out. Walt McNally survived.'

'And he's after you?'

'He don't know who I am yet, but he's wanderin' all over the territory, checkin' on every fella who's suddenly become rich in the last couple of years. The lawmen want him for a few rustlin' jobs he did, but he risks travellin' around to try and get the names of the folk who took what he reckons to be his. I'm scared to hell, and I don't care who knows it. I reckon he killed your pa.'

Tom thought about it for a moment before dismissing the idea. He told the old man about the hired killers and the behaviour of the folks in Elinor township.

'I reckon we got two different problems here,' he said finally. 'One is this McNally fella, and the other is the one what hired my pa killed. And I want *him* real bad.'

'If he's one of the high-falutin' fellas in this town of yours, you could be tanglin' with some mighty important folk. Even the lawman. You figurin' to do that?'

'If I have to.'

Tom got up and paced the floor. He had removed his spurs and the thick carpet deadened his footsteps as he moved in deep thought, while

Jethro watched through narrowed eyes.

'I was likely followed here,' Tom said after a while, 'by whoever is tryin' to keep me alive. He's probably the fella who killed my pa. This Walt McNally is another mess of mule droppings altogether. We don't know where he is, and that makes him real dangerous. But remember this, Jethro: he can't kill you until you lead him to the guns.'

The old man perked up a little. 'I never thought of that,' he admitted, 'but I know he's in town. That's why I'm scared to hell and back.'

'How do you know he's here?'

'One of Marshal Earp's deputies told me. Somebody saw his mean-lookin' face in a saloon, and reported it for the reward money. They didn't catch up with him, but he's somewhere close.'

'Old Abraham told me that my pa pulled a trick on some fella who was followin' him. It might have been this McNally character or it could have been someone from Elinor. We might pull the same trick. Are you willin' to take the risk?'

The thin man thought about it for a moment. 'It's better than sittin' around waitin',' he finally conceded.

Fourteen

Walt McNally stood quietly at the bar of the saloon with a glass of beer in his damaged right hand. His hair was cut shorter now, and the mean face was disguised with several weeks' growth of beard. He was differently dressed too, with clean shirt and a new waistcoat that boasted a neat silver watch-chain as a badge of respectability. He carried no gun and looked like a farmer in town for a quiet drink.

He was watching the large gilt mirror that graced the back wall of the saloon. Not only did it reflect his own ugly face, but it also gave him a view of the street and the closed gun store where he hoped to find the man who had stolen his army loot. He had asked about town, and learned that the new arms dealer had opened up in competition to Spangenberg only a little over two years ago. It seemed another promising lead and he was pursuing it carefully, and with dogged patience.

A young man had knocked on the door of the

gun store and finally been admitted. His face meant nothing to Walt McNally as he sipped his beer and waited to see what was going to happen next.

The young man came out after a while. He was carrying a new shotgun and some boxes of ammunition. Walt saw him shake hands with Jethro Flint in a rather formal way before going off down the street and out of sight. He went on watching the building.

Nothing happened that day, but as Tombstone grew busy early the following morning, a horse and two mules came round the corner from the corral at the back of Jethro Flint's gun store. The thin, bony frame of the store owner was seated on the small mare. His mules were loaded with food and other gear, and he steered the animals down the street towards the southern edge of town.

Walt was watching from a different position now. He was grooming his cow pony outside the barber's shop, looking to a passing deputy marshal like some innocent visitor to town. He waited until Jethro was out of sight before mounting his own horse and following quietly in the gaunt man's wake.

Jethro Flint travelled slowly, heading towards the Mexican border over a rolling plain of dried-up pasture that held little water and threw up a fine dust. He stopped in the heat of the day, had a meal, and then travelled on, unhurried and apparently not aware that Walt McNally was on his trail.

As dusk was falling, he came to a final halt on the edge of a long slope, where a small creek flowed from nearby hills towards a clump of mesquite that grew tall along the valley floor. Jethro unloaded his animals, hobbled them among the lush grass on the bank of the stream, and set out to light a fire so that he could cook his evening meal.

Walt McNally lay on his belly behind sandstone rocks about a hundred yards away. His own horse was hidden by a fall in the ground behind him and he watched enviously as he smelt the bacon frying in the skillet amid the tempting aroma of coffee.

The noises of the dark were the only sounds as Jethro settled down to sleep in the shelter of a clump of bushes that rustled steadily in the cool wind of the night. The fire gradually burnt out as a high moon paled the stars and the wind grew colder. Walt ate some dry bread and a piece of ham as he lay there. He dozed for a while and finally awoke as the sun was topping the horizon in a mist that covered the low hills.

He looked at the sleeping form in the distance and the waking animals moving slowly about in their hobbles. The mare was drinking at the creek while the two mules were nuzzling each other in happy contentment.

Walt McNally waited patiently for something to

happen. The mist began to clear from the distant hills as the sun rose hotly over the landscape. He began to sweat as a doubt crept into his mind. Jethro Flint had not moved. His horses and mules were still unharnessed, and the pile of sacks and saddlebags still lay on the ground near the creek. Something was wrong.

He stood up, drew his Colt .44, and moved quietly down the slight hill towards the recumbent figure. The mare looked up as he passed her while the mules moved a little further away at the prospect of someone expecting them to work. Walt McNally eventually stood over the sleeping man and peered down to see what was wrong.

He kicked the form with his boot, cocking the pistol as he did so. Nothing happened, and Walt swore luridly as he pulled away the rough blanket to disclose two bulky sacks and no sign of Jethro Flint.

He looked wildly around. The loads that the mules had carried were heaped next to the saddle of the mare. He checked them and swore again when he found that they contained nothing but grit and sand. Jethro had lit out during the night while Walt had dozed. The presence of the animals had lulled him into believing that a man would not decamp without his transport. He went to the edge of the creek, looking for other signs of movement. Jethro's boot marks were there, and a multitude of animal tracks that told him nothing.

The angry man walked along to the group of

mesquite that grew densely at the bottom of the slope. It was there that he found traces of other horses and mules. Somebody had met Jethro there, and they had gone off together during the hours of darkness.

Walt McNally stood undecided amid the remains of Jethro Flint's camp. He was too angry to make himself some breakfast, and too absorbed with his own troubles to realise that somebody was watching him from the brow of the slope.

It was only when he began to go in search of his own horse that he became aware of the figure that stood silhouetted against the sun with a .44 in his gloved hand. Walt blinked and raised his own Colt instinctively. He was too late and the shot took his already injured gun hand in the underpart of the wrist. He dropped the pistol with a cry of agony and then stood waiting for the final shot that would kill him.

It did not come. The man approached, slowly, and with confident authority. He picked up the fallen pistol, threw it some distance away, and stood only a couple of yards in front of the injured man.

'I thought I'd seen you before,' he said softly. 'What happened back there?'

'He's gone. Slipped away durin' the night with another set of horses.'

'He knew you were trailing him then.' The voice was full of scorn.

'I was careful, fella. Real careful.'

The man laughed harshly. 'You lost him, and you didn't even know that I was trailing you.'

Walt McNally nursed his forearm, gripping it tightly to try and stem the blood.

'I've seen you in Elinor,' he said wonderingly. 'What the hell is you doin' here?'

'Same thing you are.'

Walt shook his head. 'That can't be,' he said. 'What have you to do with army guns?'

The other man raised his head sharply. 'Army guns?' he snapped. 'We're talking about gold, man. Not guns.'

'You may be, but I sure as hell ain't interested in anythin' but gettin' back what's rightfully mine. And it ain't gold.'

Both men were silent for a moment.

'Could we be talking at cross purposes?' the stranger asked. 'Why exactly did you follow this man?'

Walt hesitated. 'I reckon that's my business, fella.'

'I'm making it mine, and I seem to have the drop on you. Now, start talking before I start shooting.'

Walt McNally talked. He told about the robbery of the army convoy and his pursuit of every suddenly-rich person in the territory. The other man listened silently, his gun never wavering as he stood immobile.

'And what about young Tom Cotter?' he asked when the story was told. 'Have you seen him?'

'Tom Cotter?'

'Jake's son. You were in Elinor when old Steve Welling went shooting at Jake. Then you followed him out of town.'

Walt's brow cleared. 'Oh, sure. Now I know who you mean. The old man went pannin' for gold so I let him be. I ain't grovellin' in sand and water to make a few dollars. I got my pride. There was a young fella called at Jethro Flint's store. He was inside for a while and came out with a shotgun. I figured him for a customer.'

'That's the man I'm after. He lodged in Tombstone but vanished during the night. My guess is that he and this Jethro met up here and went to the gold mine. That's why I followed you.'

Walt thought about it. 'Or to the army stuff,' he suggested.

'I doubt it. Where did you see Jake looking for gold?'

Walt McNally told him and the man shook his head. 'That is what Steve Welling reported back to town,' he said dismissively, 'so he was telling the truth. Jake played the same trick on the two of you that his son has played now.'

'Look, fella, you're right. You and me has been at cross purposes on this,' Walt said bitterly. 'I'm lookin' for one thing and you're lookin' for another. I reckon as how we'll both have to start again, and I've got to get to a doctor, quick. So let's call this off and go our ways.'

The other man nodded agreement. 'You have

the right of that,' he said slowly. 'The trail's cold for now.'

He levelled the gun and shot Walt McNally in the chest.

Fifteen

The wide valley was a barren place; almost a desert with the stunted groups of water-starved bushes and spikes of cactus dotted over the wide, sandy area. There was a ridge of multicoloured rock in the far distance, riddled with holes that stood out like black dots as the angle of the sun threw deep shadows into them.

It was the Nepa Valley with its old, deserted gold workings; its small streams of water poisoned by the excavations, and its only occupants the spiders and Gila monsters pursuing their prey in the arid heat.

Jethro reined in his horse and pointed to one of the mine entrances in the distant wall of rock.

'That's it, lad,' he said proudly. 'It goes in about forty feet deep and all we have to do is move out enough stuff for the mules to carry across the border. It's two days from here to Santa Rosa. We camp outside town and I go in to the local cantina for a drink. I make the contact and they ride out to meet us with the cash.'

'Can you trust them?' Tom Cotter asked.

'Sure, but we take a few precautions, all the same. We got good merchandise, and if they don't play straight, there'll be no more of it. They know that, and we're the only regular source of arms at a fair price.'

Tom looked out over the vast distance. Mexico still lay the best part of twenty miles to the south.

'Are there no border patrols?' he asked.

'Sure, but they're troops of cavalry, kickin' up one hell of a dust,' Jethro grinned. 'You can see 'em for miles. And it's one long frontier they have to cover, ain't marked worth a damn, and there are times when you can't tell which country you're in. We couldn't ask for a better set-up, lad.'

'I hope you're right.'

They rode on for an hour until they were at the base of the long rocky ridge that barred their path and presented them with sloping masses of weathered rubble from the mining. Jethro got down from his horse and began building a fire while Tom unharnessed the animals and set about helping to camp for the night.

After they had eaten, Jethro led the way up a long slope of noisy scree to the mine entrance. It was a dark opening no more than four feet high and a little less in width. He lit the lamp he was carrying and ducked to enter the tunnel.

The place was cool after the warmth of the day and every sound echoed eerily as their boots crushed the sand and gravel beneath their feet. The air was dry, with a stale, dusty smell that caught the back of the throat. Jethro halted when they had gone some twenty feet into the cliff side. The mine had widened out as gold seams had been followed and worked over the years. They saw the wooden boxes ahead of them, lit by the feeble light of the oil lamp. They filled the tunnel, piled to the roof and covered in thick dust.

'All ours, boy,' Jethro chuckled as he moved the lamp to see the expression on his companion's face. 'We'll move four cases of guns out tomorrow morning. Two to each mule. We'll fill our spare saddlebags full of ammunition, and carry a few spare saddles. That'll be enough for this trip. A quick run over the border and we'll have more than enough to live on for another six months. That's how your pa and me ran it, and it ain't never let us down.'

Tom looked at the pile of boxes. 'There's still plenty left,' he said quietly. 'That means a lot more journeys.'

'Sure does, and a lot more dollars.' Jethro looked carefully into the face of the young man. 'You ain't backin' out, is you?'

'Not exactly, but the more trips we make, the greater the risk of somethin' goin' wrong. Let's get outa here and talk about this, Jethro.'

The two men retraced their steps in silence and finally sat down in front of the fire, warming themselves in the darkening of the evening.

'You seem to be havin' second thoughts, fella,' Jethro said as he put on the coffee pot again. 'I wouldn't have reckoned you'd mind a little shootin' now and then.'

'I don't, and I've done plenty in my time,' Tom grinned, 'but just think about it. There's one hell of a lot of stuff back there, and it might take us several years to move it all. Each journey increases the risk of the army, the Mexicans, or some other fella, queerin' our pitch. Suppose we deal with it another way.'

'Such as?'

'Well, now, you tell me that nearly half the stuff is still there. There's a reward out for its recovery. That reward, with what you've already had, would set you up for life. You've got the store, plenty of money, and no worries.'

Jethro Flint poked at the fire with a piece of wood as he thought about it.

'Sounds reasonable,' he said after a while, 'but I put a lot of the money into that store, and half the reward wouldn't go very far.'

'You'd have my half as well.'

The older man stopped what he was doing. 'You mean that?' he asked. 'You'd give up your share?'

'Sure. I got a good job up north. My pa left me plenty of money, and I don't need all this to-in' and fro-in' across the border twice a year or so. Let's put an end to it, easy-like.'

'How would we explain things to the army or the county sheriff?'

'We was doin' a bit of prospectin' and came across a load of army stuff in a mine shaft. Easy as that.'

'I reckon so, but it's a hell of a thing. There's forty saddles back there, and fifty or so cavalry sabres. Them Mexicans love swords. We're talkin' about thousands of dollars, fella. No, I don't figure as how I can go along with you. We carry on as your pa and me started. Play it slow and sure like always.'

'With this Walt McNally on your tail and some fella from Elinor followin' me? That's askin' for trouble.'

Jethro kicked the fire impatiently and sent a stream of sparks flying into the night air.

'We'll meet up with them sooner or later, and that'll be the end of it,' he snapped. 'You sure ain't like your pa, son. We had this thing all worked out. What job back north could be better than a set-up like we gotten ourselves here?'

'Bounty hunting.'

There was a long silence during which Jethro's hand crept towards the gun at his side.

'That sure covers a lotta territory, fella,' he said in a very quiet voice.

'It sure does, and I make a right good livin' at it. For instance, if you was to go for that gun, I'd kill you before your finger touched the trigger.'

'Would you now? Well, I reckon as how you might at that. You're young, and you wouldn't last long at bounty huntin' if you warn't good with a gun. But I figure as how we have to part company, boy. Unless you was thinkin' of turnin' me in for the reward.'

'No. I told you what I proposed, Jethro. The army gets its gear back, you get the reward, and I goes my way.'

'Don't make much sense. What do you get out of it?'

'My pa wrote me to contact you. He said to play you fair, and I aim to do just that. I'm not after any bounties right now. I'm after my pa's killer. The one who hired him killed. That fella comes from Elinor, and I reckon to have him.'

Jethro rubbed his unshaven chin and the noise was loud in the darkness.

'Well, I can see it makes sense,' he murmured, 'but that's one hell of a lotta money we'd be turnin' away. I can't do it. Suppose we just go our separate ways? You look for your killer and I'll take a load of arms into Mexico. Got any objection to that?'

Tom grinned. 'None. I wish you the best of luck. But you're takin' risks that will get bigger the more you cross that border. My way would be easier.'

Jethro nodded. 'I know you have the right of it, Tom,' he admitted, 'but I'm too old a coyote to change habits. Let's just split up in the mornin' and part as friends.'

Tom nodded agreement and the two men settled down for the night.

*

When dawn broke over the deserted landscape, Jethro Flint found himself alone. Tom Cotter had departed as soon as his companion began snoring. He did not feel safe around a man who would go on suspecting him of betraying the hiding place to the authorities. Tom had more important things to think about than selling guns to Mexican bandits or rebels.

He camped quietly in a valley a couple of miles north of the mine area, eating a cold breakfast while he waited for Jethro to load his mules and break camp. It was late afternoon before he finally returned to the mine shaft and did what he needed to do.

Sixteen

Abraham dished out the hot food and poured coffee for the two of them. He sat down opposite Tom Cotter in the warmth of the ranch house to enjoy their meal. The oil lamp gave out a bright glow and the stove crackled as it heated a large iron kettle.

'You sure have some adventures, lad,' the old man chuckled. 'First off, you's a sheriff, then a bounty hunter. What's next?'

'Whatever it takes to get some results,' Tom grinned. 'I don't want Jethro to get hisself hurt in this. Pa wrote me to look after him, and as I see it, that means keepin' the old man from gettin' killed. That McNally fella is probably still huntin' for him.'

'He ain't around no more. The word is from town that they found his body out on the range. Somebody shot him.'

'Good, but we still gotta look after old Jethro. And we have to get this gold-huntin' craze put an

147

end to so that I can live peaceably around here.'

'So you do mean to stay put?'

'Sure do. I aim to use the money pa left me to make this a real workin' spread. And you and me will run it.'

'That sounds mighty fine, Tom. I always did want to be a top screw.'

'I warn't reckonin' on that, Abraham. I figured you as my partner.'

The old man's eyes lit up. 'Partner! Of a cattle spread? That surely is a rise in the world. I could get used to it if I tried real hard.'

'Then start tryin'. As soon as I catch up with this killer fella in town, we can begin buildin' up the spread.'

Abraham nodded as he got up to pour more coffee.

'So who is this fella?' he asked. 'You figured that out yet?'

'I think so. My pa sent me a letter to tell me to contact Jethro Flint whenever he died. My pa didn't *write* that letter.'

'That's true enough. He was like me, was your old man. Never did get more than a touch of schoolin'. Just about managed a few pages of the Blue Back spellin' book, I reckon. He went into Elinor to get that letter writ by one of his friends who could use four-legged words.'

'And he hadn't many friends in town, so which one could he trust?'

'Well – that's some question to be askin'. The

marshal, perhaps, or the money-lendin' fella at the bank. Perhaps the school ma'am or the preacher. Could be a storekeeper, maybe. There ain't many he'd trust. That's for sure.'

'And I reckon the one who wrote the letter is the killer.'

'And you know which one?'

'No, but I aim to find out. I'll lead him to the gold mine he's lookin' for.'

Old Abraham chuckled. 'A nice little trail of molasses with a trap at the end of it, eh?'

'That's right. I'll go into Elinor tomorrow and start things movin'. There's just one thing though, Abraham. I'll need your help.'

The older man straightened up and his pale eyes brimmed with moisture. 'Them's the kindest words you coulda said, lad. What do you want me to do?'

'It could be dangerous.'

'I ain't never backed down in a fight, and I ain't too old for one more shindig.'

Tom nodded. 'Then we'll get pa's killer between us,' he said grimly.

Elinor's main street was quite busy when Tom Cotter rode into town. He led a couple of mules and stopped outside one of the stores. A few glances were directed at him as his name was circulated from one person to another. The store suddenly attracted a number of extra customers as Tom purchased flour, salt, sugar, bacon, and a few other eatables as if going on a long trip.

The marshal soon heard about it, and as he came into the street, he met the banker and one of the other council men. Elijah Little's face was taut as he took Marshal Stone's arm.

'He's up to his father's tricks,' he said. 'Loading up and going to the mine. Can't you talk some sense into the lad?'

The lawman shrugged. 'If he wouldn't listen to you, what chances have I got? If he goes on like this, we'll have more killings around here.'

The council man licked his lips. 'If anybody kills him before we know where that mine is. . . !' he muttered.

'I know,' the lawman snapped, 'but what can we do? I'll try and make sure that nobody trails him from town, but I ain't got eyes in my ass. This boy's just askin' for trouble.'

The Reverend Bride came across to the little group.

'You must do your best, Marshal,' he said soothingly. 'Tom knows how bad things were here while his father was alive. I believe that I can tell you something he said to me a short time ago. He assured me that when he had visited his father's mine, and staked his own claim, he would then give the town the location so that others could make their stakes as well. The boy is no liar, and I feel that if we just wait patiently, Elinor will have its reward.'

Elijah Little pouted like a frustrated schoolboy.

'You believe that, Reverend?' he asked doubtfully.

'I do. Give the young man a chance. Let him go and stake his claim.'

The marshal nodded agreement. 'I'm inclined to go along with that,' he said as he eyed the people on the street. 'Let's break this up and try actin' normal.'

Tom came out of the store a few minutes later. People still stared at him in a hostile fashion, but the marshal was back in his office, Elijah Little had retreated to the bank, and only the preacher was able to approach the young man in a friendly manner.

'You're on your way then, Tom,' he said by way of greeting.

'Yes, Reverend. I've settled things with the three fellas that raided our spread, so now I can tackle other matters. I'm off to take a look at my pa's claim. It is a mine and he left a map with an old friend of his in Tombstone. I'll take out some gold over the next few weeks, stake a claim for myself and one for Abraham, and then it'll be open for all the folks in Elinor.'

The preacher smiled his satisfaction. 'That sounds very fair, Tom,' he said warmly, 'but watch your step. There are still folk who wish you ill. Guard your back, lad.'

'I'll do that, Reverend, and thanks for your help.'

Tom Cotter travelled slowly. His mules were heavily laden, and the weather was hot with a dry dust that caked on the skin and filled the mouth. His trail was well marked by the haze that rose from the hoofs of his animals, and there was no point in looking behind to see if he was being followed. He had no doubt that he was.

He came to the disused mine workings in the Nepa Valley on the fourth day and made camp with quiet efficiency. The hobbled animals grazed contentedly on what pasture there was while he sat before the fire and drank coffee. He was within a few yards of where he and Jethro had last camped. The dead embers of their fire were still there with the dried droppings of their mounts. He looked up at the row of mine entrances that lay at the top of the long slope and weathered scree. They were like black holes in the reddish rock, heated by the sun that was beginning to set over the distant hills.

He rose slowly to his feet, threw the dregs of the coffee away, and picked up a lantern from his little heap of mining gear. He lit it easily in the still air, and began to climb the slope to the entrance of the mine where all the army loot was stored.

Tom drew a deep breath before entering the tunnel. This was the crucial moment and he hoped that all his calculations would pay off.

As he disappeared into the dark void, the watcher drew in a sharp breath of satisfaction. He now had what he wanted and Tom Cotter was of no further use. He lay on his stomach a hundred yards from the mine entrance, the sun still warm on his back and the metalwork of the Winchester hot to the touch. He aimed the gun at the mine shaft and waited with sweat trickling down his cheeks.

It was then that a horseman came into view away to the west. He was a bulky figure against the setting sun, with a large sombrero shading his face as he reined in his mount and surveyed the scene before him. He could see the two mules, a solitary horse, and a pile of unloaded gear that lay near a dying fire. He shifted in the high Mexican saddle as he drew a rifle from its holster and rode slowly towards the camp that Tom had set up.

To the watcher, the man was a dark silhouette against the skyline, but his large spurs, the sombrero, and the broad belt of ammunition across his chest, told the world what he was. A Mexican bandit had stumbled on the scene and spotted some easy pickings at the deserted campsite.

The watcher smiled slightly. Maybe the newcomer would save him the trouble of shooting Tom Cotter. He need only wait and see. He lowered the Winchester and watched patiently for what would happen next.

The bandit advanced cautiously, glancing carefully around for the owner of the animals, and holding the Spencer rifle ready for use. He reached the fire and looked down at the pile of food and saddlery before dismounting. His body was alert for danger as he stirred the saddlebags with his foot. The watcher could hear the large spurs jingle musically as his boot prodded the sacks of flour and bacon.

The noise may also have alerted Tom Cotter. He appeared at the entrance of the mine, the lamp in his hand as he blinked in the sudden light. He hurriedly put down the lantern and went for the gun at his belt. The bandit turned at the noise of the scree as the young man moved forward. He raised the Spencer and fired almost from the hip.

The shot was loud in the quiet of the late afternoon and all the animals shied at the sudden disturbance. Tom Cotter levelled the Colt and fired two shots at the gunman. They threw up dirt near his feet as the bandit leapt aside and scrambled desperately to get the rifle to his shoulder.

He fired again and the young man stumbled to his knees. The bandit let out a yell and fired another triumphant shot that sent Tom Cotter staggering backwards. The Colt dropped from his fingers and he rolled over and over, down the long slope until he lay almost at the bandit's feet.

The man kicked the body with his boot before rolling it further down the slope into a pile of mesquite that showered dust upon it.

A silence fell again as the bandit began rounding up the mules to load the gear across their backs. He did it clumsily, not with the neat precision of an experienced mule trimmer. He muttered to himself as he worked, talking to the animals in Spanish and stopping now and then to refresh himself from a small, wicker-bound flask. When everything had been done, he looked around to make sure that he had missed nothing worth stealing. He was about to mount his own horse when he smacked the side of his head with an open hand as though remembering something important.

He hurried down to the clump of mesquite, searched the body of his fallen foe, and returned to the animals with a gunbelt, a few dollars, and Tom Cotter's silver watch.

Satisfied with the day's work, he mounted his little pony and led the other animals away from the scene. He was whistling cheerily as the little procession disappeared over the horizon in a southerly direction.

The watcher stood up and brushed the dust off his clothes.

Seventeen

The watcher strode back towards the point where he had left his large horse. He tightened the girth and led the animal over the hill and down the other side to the fire. It was all that was left now to show that Tom Cotter had been camping there. Even the coffee pot was missing. The man pulled a face at having lost the chance of a hot drink after all the hours of waiting. He tied his animal to a large bush before putting some more wood on the fire.

He looked across the slope to where Tom Cotter's body lay, sprawled amid the dust and fallen leaves. The mine was now his and nobody in Elinor was going to share it with him. He strode firmly up the scree to where the lantern sat on the gravel, still lit and hot to the touch. He picked it up carefully, the wire handle burning his hand after lying so long against the smoky glass. The man turned up the wick and bent down to enter the mine shaft.

He moved forward, feeling along the wall with his left hand and looking at the marks of the picks where veins had been followed and exploited. He breathed heavily, conscious only of his sudden luck.

Things were happening outside the mine. Tom Cotter opened his eyes and moved silently into a position from where he could view the entrance to the shaft. He saw the light disappearing and the entrance becoming dark again. He rose slowly to his feet, removing his spurs as he did so. Then he crept across to a little heap of rocks and moved a few of them aside. A length of wire sprang out like a startled snake and he took it in his hand and wiped off the dust that had clung to it. It was a fuse and he had a Vesta box in his pocket ready to light it.

The slight scrape as he made the flame sounded frighteningly loud in the still air. Tom watched as the hissing light sparked along the fuse and vanished among the scree and bits of greenery that littered the slope. He lay down and waited impatiently for what would happen next.

It did not take long. The blast shook the ground as all the army dynamite exploded and a great rush of smoke and gas mushroomed out of the mine entrance like a shot from the mouth of a cannon.

Birds that were settling for the night rose from their perches in noisy fear as the roof of the mine collapsed and a part of the rocky cliff slipped like a falling curtain to leave a great gash of brightly fresh stonework. Then everything fell silent.

The air was still filled with dust as Tom calmed down the nervous horse and loosened its girth. He checked the fire, added a little more fuel until it blazed brightly, and then sat down as if waiting for something more to happen.

He heard the noise before seeing anything. The hoofs of a horse and the whistling of a Mexican bandit were quite distinct to his listening ear. Tom grinned as the rider came into view, drawing his own animals behind him and taking off the sombrero to disclose the battered old features of Abraham. The man grinned broadly as he got down from the mount, dug out the coffee pot and started filling it.

'With all that dust about, lad,' he said cheerfully, 'I figure as how we need somethin' to loosen the throat. Everythin' go off as you planned?'

'It did, Abraham. He's inside the mine, and he ain't never comin' out.'

'Well, that's what I calls justice. And was it the fella you reckoned it to be?'

'Yes. When it came to writin' a letter to me, there was only one man my pa would trust in Elinor. And that man knew I was goin' to Tombstone to see Jethro. He didn't have to trail me there, and when I slipped away overnight, he still had Jethro and Walt McNally to follow. He sure as hell killed Walt when he found we'd led them astray. So, all I had to do was to set up this trip. He was *so* anxious to get at the gold, he got sorta blind to reality.'

Abraham chuckled. 'And we done a good job of it too, son,' he said. 'Your old pal Jethro ain't goin' to be well pleased though when he comes back here. I figure he'll be plenty mad at losin' all that army gear. There's no way he's goin' to be able to dig that lot out at his age and without help. He'll need a team of railroad layers for a mess like that.'

'He may be mad, Abraham, but he'll at least be safe. He has enough money for his old age, and he won't have folk chasin' him with guns.'

'I reckon. So now we goes home and starts raisin' cattle then?'

'Yeah, we do that, after a few cups of coffee and a little of that whiskey you got in the saddlebag.'

They set off early the next morning after rounding up their animals and loading the gear on to the mules. They also added Preacher Bride's large horse to the procession.